The Hot Wife Club

Wanda Peters

Published by Wanda Peters, 2020.

THE HOT WIFE CLUB

First edition. June 20, 2020.

Copyright © 2020 Wanda Peters.

ISBN: 979-8227533487

Written by Wanda Peters.

Also by Wanda Peters

10 Reasons You Should Cuckold Your Husband
Cruel Wife, Slave Husband
Embracing My Inner Bitch
Erotic Short Stories of Dominance and Submission
My Evil Step-Sister Returns Illustrated
Cuckolded By A Stranger, An Erotic Novel
Cuckolded By His Boss
The Hot Wife Club
Cuckolded and Bound for Punishment
Cuckolded By My Best Friend
Cuckold's Anonymous
An Anniversary To Remember
My Wife's Surprise
Terrified of Bondage A Wife in Peril
Training Her Cuckold Husband
A Little Devil in Georgia
His Mother's Advice
Addicted To High Heels or A Slave To My Wife's Boots
The Huntress
A Wedding to Remember
Evil Under a Western Sky
The Number Four Reason You Should Cuckold Your Husband
Cuckolding The Bootlicker
Bondage and Discipline 101
Tales of Love Romance and Marriage

Tales of Love, Romance and Marriage
The Evil Therapist Returns
Cracks in the Vow Six Stories of Love's Demise
Two Books Of Domination And Legal Thrillers
An Old Flame For Ava
An Interview With An Erotic Writer
Bound For Desire
The Awakening- Susan's Path to Sensual Empowerment

Title Page
The Hot Wife Club
Wanda Peters
Copyright 2015
Smashwords Edition

Chapter One: Unveiling Secrets Laura's Introduction to the Hot Wife Club

The golden sun cast a warm, hazy glow over the exclusive gathering as Laura walked in alongside her mother, Phyllis. Excitement buzzed through the air, but Laura's heart raced with anticipation and curiosity about what surprises awaited her. All Phyllis had revealed was that it was a special celebration before her upcoming wedding to the man of her dreams, leaving Laura to wonder what exciting experiences she would partake in.

As they made their way into the lavish space, Laura's eyes widened at the sight of so many scantily clad women. She couldn't help but feel a rush of nervousness and excitement at the thought of being surrounded by such beauty and sensuality. The room was filled with an intoxicating mix of elegant decor and alluring aromas, making Laura feel like she had stepped into a different world.

Noticing her daughter's flushed cheeks and wide-eyed expression, Phyllis smirked and whispered, "Wait until you see what's on the other side."

Laura furrowed her brow in confusion but followed her mother's gaze towards the opposite end of the room. There stood a tall, dark-haired man with bulging biceps and defined abs that rippled with each movement. His loincloth left little to the imagination, causing a flutter of excitement in Laura's stomach.

Before she could fully process her thoughts, Phyllis interrupted them with a sly grin. "I could arrange for you to have some private time with him later if you're interested."

Laura's jaw dropped in shock. "Mother! Have you lost your mind? I'm marrying Roger in two weeks!"

Phyllis let out a laugh. "No dear, I haven't lost my mind. Just because you've chosen one man doesn't mean you can't enjoy the attention of another, if the opportunity presents itself."

Laura couldn't believe her mother's bold words and wondered if this was some sort of test. But before she could voice her thoughts, Phyllis continued, "Your father knows exactly where we are and what we're doing. In fact, if I didn't have him locked in a chastity device, he'd probably be turned on by the thought of me being filled by another man's hard cock right now."

Laura gasped in shock, her eyes widening at her mother's blatant words. She couldn't believe this was coming from the same woman who used to scold her for even mentioning sex before marriage.

But as they took their seats and ordered drinks, Laura couldn't help but feel intrigued by her mother's newfound confidence and liberated attitude. It was as if she had shed all pretenses and expectations and embraced her true desires.

As the night went on, Laura found herself opening up to new experiences and indulging in pleasures she never thought possible. And as her mother had suggested, she chose someone worth her time and attention - the handsome man with bulging muscles who left her breathless with each touch. It was a night that she would never forget, one that taught her to embrace her desires and break free from societal expectations.

Chapter Two: Secrets Revealed The Meeting Begins

Laura took a slow, deliberate sip from her drink, allowing the warmth of the rich, amber liquid to wash over her tongue and soothe her throat. As she lowered her glass, she couldn't help but be drawn to the tall, graceful figure standing confidently at the podium. The woman's long, dark hair cascaded down her back in waves as she surveyed the audience with a cool, composed gaze. "Good Evening Ladies," she purred, her voice like silk as it wrapped around each person in the room. A faint smile graced her lips as she took in the sea of faces before her. "Welcome to our monthly meeting of The Hot Wives Club." Her words dripped with honeyed charm, captivating every listener in the room. Laura felt herself being pulled deeper into this alluring world as the speaker continued, "It is truly gratifying to see so many familiar faces in the audience tonight." Pride and satisfaction colored her tone as she spoke, gesturing towards the rows of chairs filled with women - some sitting alone while others chatted quietly in pairs. "I remember when we used to hold these meetings around a small table set for four, and yet two of those settings would often go unused." She paused for a moment, reflecting on their journey before adding, "But now look at us." Her smile widened into a beam as she gazed out at the thriving community of strong, independent women before her.

Laura couldn't help but feel a sense of belonging wash over her as she listened to the speaker's words. At first, she had been hesitant about joining this group labeled as "Hot Wives," unsure if she truly fit into their lifestyle. But now, surrounded by these supportive and empowered women, she felt like she had finally found her place.

The speaker's tone shifted slightly as she addressed any new guests in the room. "As you may have already guessed," she cautioned, her gaze sweeping over the room once more, "we will be discussing some very private matters tonight. It is of utmost importance that these stories remain confidential, so please refrain from sharing them with anyone outside of this room."

Next, she addressed the label they had chosen for themselves - The Hot Wives. "Although our group is primarily made up of married women," she mused, a playful glint in her eye, "not all of us fit into the traditional definition of those words." She paused, letting her words sink in before continuing with a hint of amusement, "If you were to look it up, you might find something along the lines of a married female swinger or a wife who has consensual sex with other men at her husband's request.' But if you were to talk to each member in this room, you would likely find that those definitions do not define our diverse lifestyles."

The speaker then posed a thought-provoking question to the room, asking how many of them were currently engaged in affairs without their husband's knowledge. As Laura looked around, she noticed about a dozen hands raised. "Quite a few," the woman remarked with a knowing smile. "Now, could I have a show of hands from those who are having affairs with their husband's knowledge?" This time, more hands went up than before.

"And of the last group," she continued, "how many of your husbands were the ones to suggest the idea of you having an affair?" Laura felt a twinge of surprise as almost every hand that had been raised in response to the previous question went up again.

The room was a striking mix of women, each one with their own unique story and experience. They shared a bond, however, of engaging in extramarital relationships. As the speaker's words reverberated throughout the space, a hush fell over the room. The air was heavy with emotion - pride, empowerment, and perhaps a tinge of guilt.

The speaker observed, her tone free of judgment or shame, "So it seems we have two distinct groups of women here. Connected only by the fact that we are all engaging in relationships outside of our marriages." She then asked the group, "By a show of hands, how many of you identify as Hot Wives?" Almost every hand in the room shot up, except for Laura's and one other woman seated across from her.

Laura couldn't help but feel both curious and slightly envious as she looked around at her fellow club members. She turned to her mother, who had also raised her hand proudly in response to the question. "Why on earth would so many women stand up and admit to having affairs?" she whispered. "And I noticed you were one of the first to raise your hand."

Her mother simply smiled and replied, "You weren't paying close enough attention when Monica asked how many of us were having sex outside of marriage at the urging of our husbands. That was one of the times I raised my hand. Now be quiet so that you do not disturb the meeting. We can talk later."

Laura was completely stunned. Finding out that her mother was having an affair was shocking enough, but discovering that it was with her father's consent and encouragement was almost too much to handle. Without another word, she got to her feet and walked away from the table, feeling overwhelmed and conflicted.

As Laura left the room, she couldn't help but wonder what her life had become. She had always been taught that marriage was sacred and that cheating was wrong, but here she was in a room full of women who openly admitted to having affairs with their husband's consent. It all seemed too surreal.

But despite her initial shock, Laura couldn't help but feel a sense of respect for her mother's honesty and bravery in sharing her truth with the group. As she walked out into the cool night air, she couldn't shake the feeling that something wasn't right about this whole situation. And yet, she couldn't deny the sense of empowerment she felt from being surrounded by these strong, confident women who were unapologetically living their truths.

Chapter Three: Rita Talmudge: The Author Uncovering Women's Secret Lives

Rita Talmadge's emotions swirled like a tumultuous storm, her mind racing as she stood in the crowded room. Her closest friend, Monica, commanded attention at the podium, and despite their friendship, Rita couldn't shake off the suspicions that had been brewing for some time now. She never expected to find out that Monica belonged to a clandestine group of like-minded women who called themselves "hotwives." This shocking revelation sent a rush of questions and doubts through Rita's mind, but amidst it all, one thing became clear: this could be the opportunity she needed to finally write a best-selling novel.

As Monica continued to speak, Rita's thoughts spun wildly. She desperately wanted to dig deeper and get the full story from her friend and as many other women in the group as possible. This could be the project that launched her career as an author into stardom. But first, she needed to convince these women to open up and trust her with their secrets.

Monica's voice cut through Rita's internal turmoil once more. "Today, we are breaking from convention," Monica announced with a sly smile. "I want you all to meet my dear friend and hopeful hotwife, Rita Talmadge." A ripple of murmurs spread through the room at the mention of Rita's name. "She may not be a hotwife...yet," Monica added with a knowing wink. "But I have high hopes that she will see the error of her ways soon enough." The room erupted into laughter and playful banter.

Monica went on to introduce Rita as an up-and-coming author who saw potential for a bestselling novel within their scandalous stories. As long as they agreed to keep their identities confidential and allow Rita creative liberties with any identifying details, participation in this project would be completely voluntary.

Rita took her place at the podium, taking a moment to survey the diverse group of women before her. From innocent-faced 18-year-olds to seasoned and fearless sixty-somethings, it was evident that this lifestyle knew no age limit.

Feeling all eyes on her, Rita began to speak. "Ladies, it is an honor and a privilege to be among such strong, intriguing, and daring women," she started, her voice ringing with sincerity. Her words were a soothing breeze, carrying a sense of comfort and understanding. "Cuckolding has piqued my interest for some time now," she continued, "but most of the literature I have come across is from the male perspective - where the husband is aroused by his wife's infidelity. However, after speaking with Monica, I learned that this is not always the case. Her husband did not react positively when he discovered her extramarital activities, which only fueled my curiosity even more. So, I am here to learn about this lifestyle from your unique perspectives as wives."

Her words struck a chord with the women in the room, their expressions ranging from intrigued to hesitant. Rita could see the internal struggle they faced between wanting to share their truth and fearing judgment from society. "I understand that this may be difficult for some of you," she addressed the group with empathy and compassion in her voice. "But I promise to protect your anonymity if you choose to share your stories with me." With a nod and a warm smile, she stepped away from the podium, leading the way to a private room that had been prepared just for them. The soft glow of candles and dim lighting welcomed them into an intimate setting, along with the comforting scent of fresh flowers and a hint of liquor in the air. "Please, feel free to join me in here," she gestured towards an open bar set up in the corner. "If you need something to calm your nerves or loosen your tongue, it's all available." Rita exuded a sense of safety and understanding, inviting the women to open up and share their truths without fear of judgment or ridicule.

Chapter Four: The Private Interviews

With a satisfied smile, Rita gracefully entered the room, pleased to see that everything was meticulously arranged according to her specifications. The bar stood proudly to the left of the entrance, its shelves overflowing with bottles of various shapes and sizes. A skilled bartender was already manning the counter, ready to mix any drink to perfection.

The space was opulently decorated with plush furnishings and rich fabrics, creating an atmosphere of luxury and comfort. The meeting area awaited, set up exactly as Rita had instructed. One large armchair sat before the wide opening at the front, facing a semi-circle of equally lavish leather chairs. The arrangement allowed for each woman's legs to stretch out comfortably in the middle if they so desired. Seven chairs were carefully placed in total, though Rita doubted they would all be filled. She knew from experience that people often avoided discussing their personal lives, especially when it involved secrets they didn't want to be revealed.

Each chair was positioned with its wide arms touching the next one, yet there was ample space between them for elbows to rest without bumping into each other. Two drink holders were thoughtfully built into the end of each arm, strategically separated so that two women reaching for their drinks at the same time wouldn't accidentally knock knuckles.

As she made her way to the bar on her high heels, the sound of polished wood echoed through the spacious room. With a sense of purpose, she ordered a tall glass of cola from the bartender, feeling slightly out of place in her role as a moderator instead of a participant. She couldn't help but wonder if some liquid courage would have been helpful for this sensitive discussion with the women gathered here.

Taking a small sip from her drink, Rita noticed the first woman entering the room. Despite expecting a younger crowd, this woman appeared to be in her late 30s or early 40s. She exuded an air of confidence and strength as she made her way towards Rita, and their eyes briefly met before the woman settled into a nearby seat. Her dark, sleek hair was pulled back into a tight bun, accentuating her sharp features and giving her an authoritative aura.

Shortly after, a second woman joined them in the room. She was younger than the first but carried herself with a maturity that belied her age. Her long blonde hair cascaded down her shoulders in perfect waves, a testament to the amount of time and effort she must have put into styling it. Rita couldn't help but admire how effortlessly glamorous she looked in head-to-toe leather, including intimidating high-heel boots that adorned her feet. It was almost as if she had stepped out of a magazine or movie scene - the epitome of a classic dominatrix.

As she closed her eyes and envisioned men crawling at this woman's feet, Rita was surprised to feel a stir of arousal deep within her own body. This had never been one of her fantasies, but something about this mysterious woman sparked a primal response within her. Shaking off the thought, she felt a hand touch her shoulder and turned to find one of the other women introducing herself with a warm smile on her face.

Monica's voice cut through the bustling room, filled with the chatter and laughter of the book club members. "Where were you?" she asked, a hint of annoyance lacing her words.

Rita shifted in her seat, taken aback by the suddenness of the question. "I am sorry," she responded, her eyes darting around the room in confusion. "I did not see you come into the room."

"Obviously," Monica retorted with a wry smile. "It is difficult to see much of anything with your eyes closed." She leaned closer, lowering her voice to a whisper. "If I didn't know better, I would think that you were deep into some sexual fantasy, lost in the alluring presence of our guests."

Rita felt her cheeks heat up at the accusation, a telltale sign of guilt she couldn't deny. "I may have been a little bit," she admitted with a sheepish grin, feeling foolish for getting caught in her own game. "But perhaps we can discuss it another time. Today is about listening to others' stories."

Monica let out a deep sigh and turned to the rest of the group, scanning their faces with disappointment. "It seems we only have a few stories to hear today," she remarked, shaking her head in disappointment. "I was expecting more members to share their tales with us."

"Well, I still haven't heard your story," Rita reminded her, hoping to change the subject and salvage the meeting. "So if you're willing, that will make three for today."

But Monica had a different idea in mind. A sly smile played on her lips as she leaned in closer to Rita. " I have a better suggestion," she whispered conspiratorially. "Why don't you come over to my house tomorrow for dinner? You can see firsthand how a dominant wife marriage works."

Rita's eyebrows shot up in surprise at her friend's bold invitation. "Are you sure that's a good idea? Won't Roy object to you airing your personal life?"

Monica let out a loud laugh at Rita's comment, causing her wine to spray out of her mouth. She quickly grabbed a napkin to wipe her lips before responding, still chuckling. "Oh no, Roy has no say in what I choose to share," she assured Rita with a mischievous glint in her eye. "And trust me, it won't be my lingerie that's being aired out. You'll want to be there for this experience. And don't worry about Roy; he's very well trained."

Despite her initial doubts, Rita couldn't help but be intrigued by the invitation now. "If you think it's all right, I'll come," she agreed, unable to resist such a unique opportunity.

"Excellent," Monica said with a wide smile. "Are you going to stay and listen to the rest of the stories?"

Rita shook her head. "No, I think the other women will feel more comfortable sharing in a smaller and more intimate setting," she suggested, glancing around at the other members still chatting in groups. "Why don't we move a few chairs so we can face them directly instead of being off to the side?"

Together, they rearranged the furniture and settled into their seats, ready for whatever stories would come their way next. The anticipation and intrigue of the upcoming dinner gathering only added to the atmosphere of the current meeting between friends.

Chapter Five: Carmen and Linda

Linda shifted her weight, the leather of her tall, stiletto boots creaking softly against the floor as she turned from Rita to Carmen. Her tight black dress hugged her curves and accentuated her fiery red hair. "So, Rita, explain to us how this is going to work. What exactly do you want us to tell you?"

Rita turned her attention to the woman draped in leather. "I'm interested in hearing about your experiences with the hot-wife lifestyle.

Not just the physical aspects, but the emotions that led you to seek intimacy outside of your marriage."

Carmen leaned forward in her plush armchair, her eyes bright with excitement. The soft glow of the dimly lit room reflected off her sleek black hair and illuminated her tanned skin. "If it's alright with you, I'll start first."

Linda gave a nonchalant shrug and nodded in agreement, her ruby-red lips forming a mischievous smile. "That works for me," she replied.

"Well," Carmen began, her voice laced with seduction, "when you mentioned sexual details, it made me reflect on my journey." She ran a perfectly manicured hand through her hair as she spoke. "At first, I thought it was simply a desire for sex that drove me towards this lifestyle. But in reality, it was the thrill of something new and forbidden that enticed me." She smiled teasingly at Rita before continuing, "Think back to when you were dating before marriage – it wasn't just the physical act of sex that brought joy, but also the excitement of getting to know someone new."

"I've never really considered that," Rita mused, her mind already racing with thoughts.

Linda, however, grinned knowingly and added, "Oh yes, I understand completely." She leaned back in her chair and crossed one long leg over the other. "Even after getting married, there is still an element of discovery between partners. And for a while, both parties are on their best behavior trying to impress one another." She gave Carmen a knowing look and asked, "How long have you been married, Rita?"

"Almost five years," she replied curiously.

"In that case," Carmen interjected, her voice dripping with seduction, "how often do you and your husband try new things together? When you go out for dinner, do you engage in stimulating conversation or find yourself drifting off into space more often?"

Both women gazed at Rita expectantly as she thought over her answer. She shifted uncomfortably in her chair, the leather squeaking in protest. She glanced down at her feet momentarily, gathering her thoughts before responding. Eventually, she decided to deflect the question and throw it back at them. "So are you suggesting that in the beginning, you weren't seeking companionship but rather something else?"

Carmen's lips curved into a knowing smile as she replied, "I admire your attempt to dodge my question." She leaned forward in her chair, her dark eyes sparkling with mischief. "But to answer yours, no, I don't think any of us went into this looking for companionship." She smirked knowingly at Linda. "I'd wager that most women in this room tonight were led down this path by their husband's fantasies – either accidentally stumbled upon or foolishly revealed." She turned to Linda and asked, "Wouldn't you agree?"

Linda's smirk matched Carmen's as she replied, her voice dripping with confidence and experience. "Oh yes, I wholeheartedly agree." She gave Rita a pointed look before continuing, "Although I am not so sure that most of them began with a husband's fantasy. Some of the ladies may have just wanted some fresh excitement in their lives." She let out a wry chuckle. "But even that stems from being bored with certain aspects of their marriages." Now it was Rita's turn to be intrigued.

"But, Carmen," she said, leaning forward in her chair, "you have my interest peaked. Why don't you tell us about the specific fantasy your husband had that led you to become a hot wife?"

Carmen paused, considering how much to reveal. She ran a hand through her hair and took a deep breath. "All right, I will try to give you the abbreviated version." She gave a half-smile and a wink. "Otherwise, we could be here until midnight and I still wouldn't get to see my lover tonight."

Her nonchalant tone surprised Rita but also piqued her curiosity even more. "Please feel free to share as much or as little as you'd like," she said eagerly. "You already have me captivated."

Rita waited patiently for Carmen to continue. She had a feeling this was going to be a very interesting story indeed. "Well, as you might have guessed," Carmen began, her voice taking on a sultry tone, "it all started when I was at a somewhat low point in my marriage." She leaned back in her armchair, her body relaxed and confident. "My husband and I had been together for many years, and we had grown apart in so many ways." Her eyes flickered with sadness before they hardened with determination. "We never seemed to have the same chemistry we used to. At least, not in the bedroom."

One hot summer day, when the sun was high and the birds were singing, my husband surprised me with a bold proposition - he wanted us to visit a professional dominatrix together. I could see the signs of nervousness on his face, but his eyes sparkled with excitement. As I processed his words, I couldn't help but feel a rush of curiosity. My husband and I had always been open-minded, but this was uncharted territory for us. The thought of experiencing something new and intimate with him sent shivers down my spine.

"We began to explore the world of BDSM together, attending parties and events, and even signing up for a few classes. We quickly discovered that this lifestyle wasn't just about dominance and submission; it was a way to rekindle our connection and reignite the passion that had been missing in our marriage for far too long. As I got more involved, I found that I loved the idea of being in control, of being desired by multiple men, and of exploring sexual fantasies that I had never even considered before. It gave me a sense of power and confidence that I had never felt before. I was hooked."

Chapter Six: Carmen's Story

"I am sure you have noticed that I am somewhat older than you two. The reason I mentioned that is because my generation typically took their marriage vows more seriously than many do today. I was married in a church and took standard vows. 'Do you promise to love, honor, cherish, and protect him, forsaking all others and holding unto him, for as long as you both shall live?' When I said I do to that, I meant it and had no intention of ever sleeping with another man. And I have to tell you that I was exceedingly happy with that arrangement for the first 15 years of my marriage."

"So, I guess I need to ask what changed?" asked Rita.

"I guess we both did to differing degrees. Now it was true that sex with Herb became less and less enjoyable. Looking back, it is easy to put my finger on the reasons, no pun intended." She gave a little giggle. "When we were dating, and the first few years of marriage, he worked hard to make sure that I was satisfied sexually. He would spend hours massaging my feet, legs, and back while gently planting soft kisses over various parts of my body. At first, his ministrations relaxed me from head to foot, and then he would use those same hands to arouse me, first my breasts and nipples and then between my legs. And he was a master at giving oral sex. My God, did that man know how to use his tongue? By the time he got around to penetrating me with his cock, I was so wet and hot that I was ready to explode with orgasm before he had even taken a full stroke."

"Wow, that sounds like it would have been heaven. I am a little jealous. I have only been married for five years, and I have never experienced anything like that with my husband."

"Really," Linda chuckled. "Perhaps we will have a new member of the Hotwife's Club shortly."

"Yeah, well, I would not count on that anytime soon. I don't find sex to be the most important part of being married." Rita pointed out.

"And what is it that makes you think that sex is the driving factor for the people in the other room?" Asked Linda. "I am sure it plays a part in their lives as it does in mine, but not the largest or most important part; I would bet. Carmen, why don't you continue with your story?"

"Well, as I was saying, in the beginning, he spent a lot of time making sure that I was completely satisfied in the sex department. While that was going on my emotional needs were being met as well. When he would come home from work, the first thing he would do would be to take me into his arms for a big hug and a kiss, and he never left the house without kissing me goodbye. Everywhere we went together; we held hands. And he never forgot any of the special occasions, birthdays, anniversaries, or Valentine's Day.

Carmen paused and took a sip from her drink. "But then things started to change, little things at first like forgetting to kiss me goodbye before he left for work. And then he started walking a little behind or in front of me, not holding hands."

"And I bet the sex changed as well, did it not?" asked Linda.

"Of course, if he was no longer as interested in the small intimate things that made us so close emotionally, then he no longer cared as much about making me happy in bed. The massages got shorter and shorter until they disappeared altogether. His oral ministrations became nonexistent, and my orgasms became few and far between."

"Did you try talking with him about it?" Asked Rita.

"Sure, and do you know what he told me? The honeymoon can't last forever."

"So was that when you decided to seek sex outside of marriage?" Rita asked.

"No, that was when I decided to try even harder to get my husband's attention. But I am afraid that the story will have to wait for another time. My new lover is waiting for me in the bar." As she turned to leave, she handed Rita a business card. "Give me a call sometime during the week. We can set up a time for you to come to the house and interview Harold. I am sure he will love to tell you how it feels to be a cuckold."

Chapter Seven: Meanwhile at Rita's House

The blonde woman begged for mercy, her hands bound tightly behind her back as she pleaded with Ray to stop their sadistic game. "This is sick and twisted," she sobbed, tears streaming down her face. "If my sister finds out, she'll cut off your manhood and force-feed it to you."

Ray's dark eyes twinkled with a sinister joy as he observed Charlene, naked and bound to the worn wooden desk. The cube-shaped room, bathed in the dim glow of a single hanging bulb, echoed with her whimpers and pleads for mercy. But his sadistic desire was just too robust to be tempered – the sight of her helplessness only fueled his primal hunger.

"Make your pick," he demanded, presenting her with two wicked choices: a paddle made of polished cherry wood or a tawse crafted from thick leather. The fear in her eyes did nothing but stoke the fire within him, igniting an insatiable thirst that could only be quenched by her surrender.

She breathed falteringly, glancing between the objects of torment, and finally whispered, "The tawse." Ray's lips curled into a devilish grin, his shaft twitching at her submission. He strutted back towards her, his cock rigid and throbbing urgently.

Her body trembled on the rough doormat spread across the desk. She winced when she felt it against her raw nipples; it was coarse and painful. Yet there was an erotic thrill about this blend of pain and pleasure which coiled tightly inside of her like a spring ready to release anytime.

Without warning, Ray dove headfirst into the heat between her legs. His tongue traced her sensitive folds before lapping up her slick arousal. Her gasp echoed off the walls, bringing an arrogant smirk onto his face as he continued his oral assault until she was writhing beneath him, begging him to fill her.

He obliged willingly. Guiding himself to her center, he slowly pushed his hardened length inside her soaked core. With each delicious inch he claimed, she couldn't resist moaning his name desperately while biting down on her lower lip. There was no denying how wet this ordeal had made her; every thrust into her plush depths was met with a lewd squelch that echoed around the room.

The first hit from the tawse landed on her bare shoulders, drawing a sharp cry from her lips. The leather stung against her supple skin but it did nothing to quench the carnal flame that had been ignited within her. In fact, it only made her more needy. She squirmed, desperate for release.

Ray continued his brutal rhythm – thrusting and spanking – until she was gasping and pleading. Her soft pleas only egged him on further; he filled her over and over again, leading them both closer to their inevitable climax.

When it finally happened, it was an explosion of sensations. A symphony of moans echoed through the room as they surrendered to their torturous pleasure. He pumped his seed inside her as she convulsed around him, welcoming every hot spurt.

Afterward, he admired the reddened marks on her body with a sated smile before releasing her from the restraints. It would be days before these would fade, serving as reminders of their wicked escapade. "No pleasure without pain," he reminded her once again before hinting at the ultimatum she faced - choosing between two men in very different ways.

Her heart filled with despair knowing there'd be no compromise with Ray. And if she wanted to continue this illicit affair, she would have to convince Jason to make unimaginable sacrifices.

"Then I guess this is goodbye," Ray said coldly. "I enjoyed our little sessions. Now get out of my house." She left, feeling used and torn between love and lust, wondering if she had made the right choice in pursuing this dangerous liaison with Ray.

Chapter Eight: Linda's Story

Linda walked to the bar to refill her glass as Carmen took her leave. The stacked bare-chested barman smiled at her as he took her glass. Linda smiled back and licked her lips, her eyes moving down to the loincloth covering his private parts. Seeing a slight tent beginning to form rewarded her.

"What can I get for you, Mistress?" He asked.

"Right now, another Margarita. Perhaps a very large piece of meat later if you have such a thing."

The barman smiled and reached down and pulled the loincloth away from his body, allowing his gigantic cock to spring free. "Would this suffice, Mistress?" He said with a large smile on his face.

"What time do you get off work?"

"A few minutes after you folks finish with the room." He answered.

Linda wet her lips again and then handed him the key to her room. "Room 407. I will expect you naked and on your knees when I come up."

"It will be my pleasure, Mistress." He said as he handed the refilled glass to her.

Linda was chuckling a little to herself as she returned to her seat across from Rita.

"I guess you made a new friend," Rita remarked as Linda sat down.

"Dear Lord, you should see the size of his cock. I may have a little trouble walking in the morning, but it will be well worth any discomfort he causes me tonight."

"Aren't you afraid of catching something?"

"Not at all. All of the males who work here are tested regularly, and I insist that they use condoms."

Linda noticed that Rita shook her head slightly. "You do realize that you will not get many interviews if you insist on judging our lifestyles?"

"I apologize and beg your pardon. It is just that this is so new to me."

"If you don't mind me asking, why did you decide to write a book about something you have no first-hand knowledge of?"

"Writers do not need first-hand knowledge of a subject to write about it. They just need to do the research. For example, a writer does not have to be a serial killer to write about one. But talking to a serial killer might be helpful."

"So, I guess I am your serial killer for the moment? Where would you like me to start?"

"Why not tell me about the first time you decided to take a lover and why?"

As I begin to share my story, I realize that in order for you to truly understand it, we need to go back further. Before I was married, I was what some may call sexually active. I wasn't easy, but I enjoyed the thrill of being pursued by boys. Being wined and dined was the ultimate flattery, and I couldn't get enough of it.

Then Ronald came into my life, and suddenly love became a warm and fuzzy feeling rather than just a concept. He was charming, funny, and had enough money to take me out in style. After a few months of exclusive dating, he asked me to marry him, and without hesitation, I said yes. The honeymoon phase seemed like it would last forever, but reality soon set in.

Within a couple of years, both Ron and I were bored with our sex life. We still engaged in it regularly, but it lacked effort and passion. That's when Ron came up with the idea of "Date Night." He would drop me off at a bar and wait outside or drive around before coming in to try to pick me up as if we were strangers both looking for some fun.

The first time we tried this, Ron didn't even wait long before coming inside. It was clear that neither of us were fully invested in the act. But after a few drinks, we decided to head home. Playing along with the stranger fantasy, I pretended not to know him and ended up having incredible sex. That's when I knew that this could spice things up in our relationship; I just needed Ron to agree to it.

And sure enough, he did suggest doing it again the following Friday night. But this time, I added a twist - he would pick out my outfit for the evening. Not only that, but he would also buy me a brand new lingerie set along with a short and sexy dress, a sheer blouse, and a pair of "fuck me" pumps. I could tell he was uncomfortable with the idea, but he agreed to it.

On Friday night, Ron took it a step further and insisted on bathing and dressing me before we went out. And just to add to his discomfort, I made him trim my pubic hair as well. As I watched him nervously snip away at my hair with shaking hands, I couldn't help but feel a warm sensation in my pussy, knowing that this was arousing for both of us. It was an incredibly exciting thought - the possibility of another man enjoying my trimmed bush.

Of course, at that point, I didn't have any concrete plans to take a lover. But the idea alone was enough to turn me on beyond belief.

Linda stopped her discourse at that point to take another drink and gather her thoughts, but Rita did not interject any ideas or ask any questions. She was completely absorbed into the account of Linda's story, and she did not want anything to get in the way of it continuing.

Linda drained her glass and held it up as a sign for the bartender to come with a refill. She did not doubt that he would remember exactly what it was she was drinking or that he would love to serve her by bringing the drink to her seat. She smiled to herself as she watched him walk across the room to her, not even trying to hide the large tent in his loincloth. "I see you are looking forward to our meeting," Linda said as she moistened her lips with the tip of her tongue.

"Very much so, Mistress. I hope that I may serve you in very special ways later."

"I am sure you will." She then turned to Rita. "Do you care for anything from our servant? I am sure he would be happy to serve you as well."

"I am fine for now." Rita did her best not to dwell on the double entendre. But not being blind, she had noticed the bulge extending from his groin, and it took all her discipline to keep from thinking about what was causing it.

The rear view was almost as good as the front view, and neither woman spoke until he had returned behind the bar.

"I guess I better continue with this tale before I give him my tail." Linda laughed. She then took another long drink from her glass before resuming the story.

"So after I had allowed him to prepare me for a date, I had him drive me to a bar that we had been to before. It had a nice little dance floor and a band that played a variety, including slow dance music. I set the alarm on his phone for one hour and told him that he was not allowed to come into the bar until the alarm went off. This time I was going to make sure that I had at least enough time to find a good-looking guy and spend a little time flirting with him.

As I entered the bar, I took a few minutes to allow my eyes to adjust to the relative darkness. But as I looked around, my pupils must have expanded to new limits. For everywhere I looked, there were good-looking men and practically no women. I was like a kid in a candy store. Which one should I try first?

I made my way to the bar and deliberately caused my nylon-clad legs to brush against each other so that the nylon would make that sexy swishing sound. Of course, in the noisy bar, I was probably the only person who could hear it, but it made me feel good regardless. I might have even allowed my hips to sway a little more than I usually would as a form of advertisement that said here I am; I can be had.

I was not sure exactly what I was going to do, but I settled onto an open bar stool allowing my skirt to slide up my legs without trying to adjust it back down towards my knees. Completely unladylike, I opened my legs slightly, providing a small view of my panties to anyone who might care to look. A few of the male patrons had decided that the view was interesting because I had hardly sat down before three of them were surrounding me, asking if they could buy me a drink.

Well, I could bore you with the details of what I chose to drink but suffice it to say that by the time that Ronald showed up, I was well on my way to a buzz. I was so engrossed in dancing with each of the men that I did not see Ron come into the bar. But he saw me, and it did not take him long before he rushed across the room to lay claim to his wife. The band was playing a slow number, and one of my newfound friends, Phil had me locked in his arms as he swayed my body to the music. I had not objected when he had dropped his hands from my waist to my buttocks, nor did I protest as he drew my hips firmly against his. The only thing that kept me from being fucked on the dance floor was the layers of cloth we wore.

I had nuzzled my face against his chest and had closed my eyes. I am sure that I must have been purring like a kitten being stroked. I know that some sounds of pleasure were escaping my lips. I wanted that dance to go on forever.

But it was obvious that Ron was not as pleased. I felt my newfound playmate being ripped from my arms as my eyes flew open to see a very livid husband accosting my partner. 'Get your filthy hands off my wife!' he demanded as he cocked his fist back. As I tried to intervene, everything seemed to slow down into slow motion. I could see Ron throwing the punch at Phil, but I had moved into the path of his fist. The next thing I knew, I was on the floor, and a few seconds later, Ron joined me there.

Needless to say, the three hunks of love disappeared shortly after announcing that they were not there to play our sick games.

That put an end to "date night" for a while after that.

"Okay, then how did you get from there to here?" Asked Rita.

"I am afraid the rest of the story will have to wait until another time. It is getting quite late, and I did promise to meet someone in my room." She reached into her purse and produced what appeared to be a business card. "My cell number is on the back. Give me a call, and we can plan another time to continue this story."

With that, Linda got up, excused herself, and walked out of the room. Rita sat there for a few minutes more until the bartender came over and asked if there would be anything further that she desired. Realizing that he was hoping she was done with the room for the evening, she told him no and proceeded to follow Linda out of the room.

Chapter Nine: Emma and Her Bootlicking Husband

As Rita again entered the main meeting room, Monica met her halfway across the floor. A tall, shapely brunette who was wearing a bright red dress and red heels accompanied her.

"I hope that you got the stories that you were looking for," Monica stated.

"Well, I certainly got the beginning of some interesting material but not the full picture I was hoping for. But then I guess I should not have expected a complicated subject such as this to be covered completely in just one sitting."

Monica turned to the black-haired beauty standing beside her. "Rita, I would like you to meet Emma. She has a story that she said she would be willing to share with you. If you don't have to rush home to be with your husband, that is."

"I told Ray that I would be late getting home tonight and to not wait up for me, so I would be more than happy to hear your story."

A burst of laughter escaped Emma's lips, and Monica joined in with a few soft chuckles. "Okay, ladies, what is so amusing? Or is it a private jest?" Rita queried, eyes sparkling with curiosity.

"It was your remark about telling your husband not to wait up for you," Emma replied with a grin. "You may not know this, but nearly every woman here tonight has said the same thing. Of course, most of them aren't spending their evening chatting with another woman."

"Ah, so I take it your husband won't be waiting up for you either?"

Emma's smile grew wider. "Oh, he'll be waiting all right. And I highly doubt he'll be getting any sleep until I come home." She fished out her smartphone from her purse and deftly navigated through the menu before handing it to Rita.

Rita took her time studying the photo that adorned the front of the phone. It depicted a man bound to a tall kitchen stool, completely naked except for a black leather hood covering his head and a leather harness tightly secured around his upper body. His arms were twisted painfully behind his back, and his ankles were pulled up and tied to the top rung of the stool. Rita couldn't help but notice how taut his calf muscles looked from the strained position. She wondered what would happen to him if the stool were to tip over - until she noticed that a rope was tied from the harness to the ceiling, presumably as a safety measure. Should the stool topple, the rope would prevent the man from falling and injuring himself. As she went to hand the phone back, she caught sight of something that hadn't registered with her at first - the man's manhood encased in some kind of metal tube and his testicles wrapped with what appeared to be a delicate chain of jewelry.

Rita's hand trembled slightly as she returned the phone to Emma's outstretched hand. "I assume that's a photo of your husband waiting for you at home?"

Emma seemed to scrutinize Rita's expression for a moment before responding. "Yes, it seems you're quite shocked."

"I suppose I'm just worried about his safety. What if something were to happen while he's all tied up and alone?"

"Who says he'll be alone? There's always someone in the house with him when I'm not there - whether he's bound or not. Tonight, for example, his brother is babysitting for me. Other times, his mother will stay over, or perhaps one of his sisters will take care of him. And if no one else is available, I'll even ask my husband's secretary to keep an eye on him."

"My God, the poor man must be completely humiliated. Does everyone he knows realize how you treat him?"

"I am not sure you are really up to hearing this story. Were you as judgmental with Carmen and Linda as you are with me?"

"I am sorry if I sounded judgmental. I guess I am just shocked that a wife would subject her husband to such humiliation. I would love to hear how all this started, and I promise to keep any further thoughts to myself. How long have you been married?"

"A little over a year. I know that sounds like a short time, and I suppose it is compared to most of the other women who belong to this club, but I found out even when we were on our honeymoon that something was a little off with Herb. Oh, he was willing enough to make love to me on our wedding night, but his ardor waned fast thereafter. For the entire week, we made love a total of three times, and I initiated the action in the last two.

Once we got back home, he seemed to lose interest in sex altogether. I figured that there was something wrong with me; that I did not measure up to his expectations in some way. I tried buying new lingerie, rented sex tapes, and suggested counseling, but nothing worked.

Then one day I came home early from work. I figured that I would surprise him when he got home by meeting him wearing nothing but a pair of high heels. Well, imagine my surprise when I pulled into the driveway and found that his car was already parked there. I was a little pissed off that even my attempt at blatant seduction was thwarted as I opened the front door and thought about calling out to let him know that I was home. But, something told me that stealth was the better plan so I closed the door as quietly as I could and removed my heels so that they would not make a clicking sound on the hall tile.

The bedroom door was partially open. I guess he figured since he was alone in the house that closing the door was not mandatory. I looked through the crack, and I could see him in the mirror. He was lying in the middle of the bed, stark naked. He had his left arm inside of one of my tall black boots, and he was holding it up to his mouth. His other hand held a pair of my panties and his rock-hard cock. My mouth must have fallen to the carpet as I watched his tongue sneak out and swipe across the toe of my boot. He let a moan escape from his lips as if he was in sexual ecstasy. My first thought was to throw open the door and start screaming. My second thought was to take out my smartphone and document what he was doing for use later. My sane mind won out, and I gently eased the door open and raised my camera. He was so enthralled in his deviant behavior that he did not even notice I was there until I had a half dozen incriminating photos of him licking my boot as he stroked his cock.

Only then did I fully enter the room and walk to the bed. With everything I had, I knocked that boot off his arm with my first blow, and then I knocked the look of surprise off his face with the second.

So tell me, Rita, what would you do next if you were in my position?"

Rita hesitated since she had not been expected to be put on the spot. After all, she was the one conducting the interview. "I am not sure. I would probably have gone someplace to calm down, and then I would have confronted him and demanded an explanation."

"Really?" Emma asked. "Your husband has not shown any interest in you sexually, and then you come home and find him making love to your boot, and all you want is an explanation?"

"Okay, I guess I would want to kill the son of a bitch, but I am not the violent type. So tell me, what did you do?"

"I am not proud of it, but you have to understand that I was hurt. It was bad enough when I figured that there was something wrong with me but then not even to measure up to an inanimate object like a boot. I wanted him to hurt the way that I did, and so I sent those pictures to the one person that I knew he would not want to see them. I sent them to his mother."

"Oh my. I bet that caused some sparks to fly."

"Yes, but not quite the way I had expected. Only a few minutes passed before my phone rang, and his mother was on the other end. She informed me that we needed to talk and suggested that we have drinks at her house. I asked her if she wanted me to bring her bootlicking son with me. She told me that she would handle Herbert herself later, but for tonight she wanted to talk with me. The one thing that bothered me was that she seemed to be so unbelievably calm. I thought for sure that she would be either pissed at me for sharing our private dirty laundry or devastatingly angry at Herb for getting caught in such a compromising position.

She told me not to worry about Herb and that she would take care of him, but for the present, she wanted to make sure that I was okay. So I agreed to meet her at her house.

I was still apprehensive as I entered her front door, but she quickly set me at ease by opening her big arms and drawing me into a big hug. At that point, the dam opened, and my entire body was wracked with huge sobs, and tears flowed freely from my eyes. By the time I had cried myself out in her arms, the entire front of her bodice was soaked with my tears. Only when I had composed myself to a degree did she lead me into her living room and sit me down on the sofa. She left me for a minute to go get me a strong drink and then came back and sat beside me. Again she put her arm around me and pulled me tight to her breast."

Rita now needed a minute to digest what she was hearing, but she did not dare interrupt the tale for fear that it would lose some of the power that she felt from it. Emma could see something in Rita that made her stop and ask if she was all right. "Yes, perfectly fine, I assure you." was Rita's answer. "I am just amazed that a man's mother would care so very much for her daughter-in-law that she would welcome her into not only her house but her arms after that woman had sent her such a terrible set of pictures of her son."

"Yes, and frankly, it surprised me as well, but I had bottled up my feelings for so long that Liz's comfort was about the only thing that kept me sane at that time. Finally, I composed myself enough so that when she asked me to tell her the whole story, I was able to relate it in some detail. I told her about the honeymoon and about my increasing frustrations with trying to get her son to be intimate with me. She listened without interrupting once while I railed about how badly her son had treated me. When I finally told her that the worst part was, that I did not have any idea why he did not find me attractive, only then did she speak.

'Let's find out.' she declared. I found out later that she was calling her other son, Harold. Within an hour he arrived leading a very scared, bound, and hooded Herb into the room. No words were spoken as Herb was stripped of his pants and underpants and secured over the back of a tall wooden chair. His mother then handed me a large wooden hairbrush and a cue card. On the card were instructions and some sample questions that I might use to interrogate my husband. The first rule on the card was that I was not to disclose who else was in the room but to tell Herb that others were present. The second rule was that I was to give Herb 5 hard strokes on his bare bottom with the hairbrush before I started questioning him. I gladly followed that instruction. I took the brush and walked quickly across the room. Taking a stance to the left of Herb, I raised the brush and brought it down with all my might across both of his ass cheeks.

His scream of pain was muffled somewhat by the leather hood he wore, but his jerking and trying to pull himself away from me told me I had struck some pretty sensitive nerves. I saw him tensing up and trying to prepare himself for another blow, so I deliberately waited until I saw his ass muscles relax before I brought another blow, down in a slightly different spot. This time even the hood could not muffle his scream, and I felt a small amount of moisture begin to form between my legs. I looked over at his mother and brother to see what their reaction was and was gratified to see both of them with a smile on their face."

The scene was so vivid in Rita's mind that she felt as if she was there watching that brush, land on bare flesh. And although she had never thought of herself as having a cruel or sadistic streak, she felt a small amount of moisture forming between the lips of her pussy. But then Emma was continuing with her story.

"So I continued with another three very hard strokes enjoying each one to the fullest. Finally, I stepped back and addressed my now sobbing husband.

"Herb, we are not alone in this room, although I am not at liberty to say who else is present. You have been brought here to answer some questions for me. If you answer quickly and honestly, you will not be hurt. Every time you try to lie to me or attempt to avoid giving me a truthful answer, you will get another five strokes similar to the five you just received. Do you understand what I have just told you?

Herb muttered something that I was not able to understand, and I knew that the hood would have to come off if I was to obtain the information that I sought. So I went to his mother and explained my dilemma. She left the room but returned shortly with a long thick scarf. I immediately knew what she had in mind, so I went to Herb and removed the leather hood from his head, but before he had a chance to look around, I wrapped the scarf around his head covering his eyes. I tied it securely in place and then stepped back behind him and repeated my instructions. This time his answer of yes ma-am was clear and distinct.

I was pleased that he called me ma-am for some reason. I guess it was the first time in some months that I felt that he respected me. So I asked him the first question that came to mind. When I came home and found you on the bed, you had a pair of my panties in one hand and one of my dress boots in the other. I assume that the nylon of the panties felt good against the skin of your cock, but why were you licking my boot?

Herb hesitated, trying to find a way to answer without too much embarrassment, I assumed. But I was not going to allow that to happen. And you will recall I had warned him. So I stepped close to him and brought that hairbrush down with everything I had, this time right where his legs joined with his ass. There was nothing to muffle his scream this time, and I was afraid that the neighbors might hear him. I looked to his mother for advice, and she just motioned for me to continue, so I gave him four more strokes as hard and as fast as I could.

I have learned a lot about administering punishment since that day, and I probably should have taken more time in between strokes, but at that time, I was looking for answers more than I was looking to hurt him.

Now Herb, answer the question, why were you licking my boots?

'It is a fantasy of mine. I like to pretend that I am your slave and that you order me to do humiliating and degrading things. When I am alone, licking your boots is about as degrading a thing as I can come up with.'

Well, I was completely stunned. I had no idea that Herb wanted me to sexually dominate him, and I would not have thought of telling him to lick my boots in a million years. The very idea was completely disgusting to me. Just the thought of kissing the man after watching him lick the filth off my boots made me want to vomit. Finally, I composed myself enough to continue with my interrogation.

So all this time, when I was trying to get you to make love to me, you were fantasizing about me forcing you to do disgusting things? Were you unable to perform, or did you just not want to be intimate with me?"

'I wanted you to force me to do whatever you wanted.' The way he was tied, his head was already hanging down, but I could see it drop just a little more as he said it.

I thought for a minute whether there was anything I wanted from this pathetic excuse for a man. My first inclination was to walk out of that house and go directly to my lawyers and file for divorce. How could I live with someone that I had to force to make love to me? But then it dawned on me that perhaps I could have the best of both worlds.

So you want me to order you around and make you do things for you? I asked him. Without hesitation, he told me that would make him the happiest man in the world.

Then how about you start doing all of the housework?

He told me that he would be willing to do as much as he could, but he wasn't sure if he could do it all and still maintain a full-time job.

My first inclination was to agree with him. But then I realized that I was doing almost everything around the house including the cooking and I was working full time so why in hell couldn't he? Here's the thing, I told him. I will make a schedule for you. Some things will need to be done every day, like making our beds, sprucing up the bathrooms, preparing meals, and cleaning up after them. Other things might not have to be done quite so often. But you will be doing all the housework. From now on, I won't lift a finger unless I am in the mood, and I promise you I won't be in the mood very often. And if for some reason, you are not able to get everything done before your normal bedtime, then you will just have to lose a little sleep. Are you in agreement with what I have told you so far?

I swore I heard a little moan escape from his lips, and I went over and walked to where I could observe his cock, and sure enough, it was standing straight up and twitching. For some reason, that pissed me off, and I picked up that brush and gave him a whack right between his legs. I was very happy when I saw his little penis shrivel up and almost pull back into his body.

Now answer the question, worm. Do you agree to the stipulations I have laid out for you so far?

'Yes, ma-am,' he replied.

Very well then, here is the second thing that you need to agree to. Since I have gone for the last year with practically no sexual release, I think it is only fair that you go for the next year without an orgasm. I am not sure how I am going to ensure that you don't play with yourself, but I am sure someone can help me find a way.

At that point, his mother beckoned to me to follow her out of the room. When we were alone in the kitchen, she bent close to me and quietly said. If you want to guarantee that he doesn't play with himself, I have just the thing for you. Wait here, and I will be right back."

Once again, Emma took a break to take a few sips from her drink. Rita used that time to try wand compose herself as she was, for some reason, becoming quite excited by listening to this woman's story of how she began to dominate her husband. By this time, there was enough moisture pooling in her panties so that she was afraid that the other two women would smell her musk. So she excused herself to powder her nose as the saying goes. In the restroom, she pulled off the now very wet panties rolled them up in some paper towels, and stuffed them in her purse. As quickly as she could, she used some toilet paper to dry herself between her legs and then used the deodorant that she always carried to mask the smell before returning to the room.

"So, what idea did your mother-in-law have for you?" Rita asked.

"Well, I could not believe it. She came back into the room and handed me a curved metal tube connected to a metal ring by a small padlock. I looked at it, trying to figure out what it was or how it could be used, and finally, she told me it was a chastity device. I asked how she came to have one readily on hand, and she smiled and told me that was a story for another day. I asked her how it went on, and she said that it was best if she showed me. We then went back into the living room to put it on, Herb.

He did not resist as we untied him and turned him around so that we had better access to his genitals. His mother knew exactly what she was doing with the device, and within a matter of two minutes, it was fitted and locked. I expected that she would give me the key, but instead, she tucked it into the pocket of her dress. Later she told me that she wanted to make sure that I did not have sympathy for Herb and release him before he learned to control himself.

Liz then suggested that Harold take Herb home and get him started on doing a long night of housework. She had even prepared a list of chores that needed doing in every room that usually got delayed, including cleaning out the refrigerator and cleaning the oven. And then she sent Herb on his way. But she wanted me to stay a little longer as she had something important to talk with me about."

"Really," Rita queried. "I wouldn't think that there would be much more to say at that point. You had already gotten an agreement on the two major points of contention."

"Yes, well, Liz knew that there was still a bone of contention that needed to be addressed."

"And that was?" asked Rita

"My lack of sexual fulfillment. While denying Herb an orgasm for a year might be gratifying to a degree. It did nothing for my frustrations. And Liz was perceptive enough to realize that. So she gave me a suggestion that I had not even considered. She told me that I should take a lover."

"You are kidding me? His mother suggested that you cheat on her son?"

"I know that it sounds strange, but later I learned that Liz had cuckolded Herb's father many years before that. And she said it was the best thing she had ever done for her marriage. You see, if a wife is not happy with the sexual aspect of marriage, she cannot be happy with any aspect of marriage. But I should let Liz tell you that story herself. She is a member of the club, and I am sure you will meet her at some point in time."

Rita pondered what she had learned for a moment and then asked another question of Emma. "So how long after that did you take a lover, and how did Herb react, or did he know?"

Emma had a huge smile on her face. "Herb eventually knew. But not for some time. And truthfully, looking back, I kind of wished that I had kept him in the dark entirely."

"Why do you say that?" Asked Rita.

"It may sound strange, but it is just more fun sneaking around having an affair than it is going out with your husband's knowledge. Of course, I know a lot of the other women will tell you just the opposite. I have talked to a lot of them who believe that having their husbands know what they are doing is a real turn-on, and some of them enjoy the fact that their husbands are suffering mentally, knowing that their wife is having sex with another man. One even told me watching her husband being humiliated by her lover was better than the sex act itself."

With a sly smile, Rita leaned in closer to Emma and asked, "Do you use your lovers to humiliate your husband?" The low hum of the bar filled the momentary silence as they both took a sip of their drinks.

Emma's response came easily, "Oh, God, yes. I make sure when I get home to tell Herb all about my date and make sure he knows how much bigger the man's cock is than his. And I always toss him my soiled panties and tell him to sniff and taste the crotch, so he will know what a real man tastes like."

Rita's eyebrows raised in surprise. "Pardon me, but I don't see why a man would stay with a woman who treats him that way."

A mischievous grin played on Emma's lips as she replied, "You should probably ask Herb that question, but I think I know what his answer would be."

"Really? And what answer do you think he would give?"

A playful glint entered Emma's eyes as she explained, "Herb would say I don't know why a man would stay with a woman that doesn't. You see, Herb loves me so much that he wants me to be happy. He knows that I deserve to have sex with a real man, and Herb is convinced that he is not a real man. But don't take my word for it; feel free to talk with him yourself." She reached into her purse and pulled out a business card, handing it to Rita. "Here is a card with his number on it. Give him a call and set up a meeting. I will instruct him to answer your questions honestly. He knows better than to disobey me." A proud smirk crossed her face before she added, "But for now, you will have to excuse me. I have something big, hot, and hard waiting for me."

As Emma left the bar, Rita looked at her watch and saw that it was well past midnight. She turned to Monica, who had been silently observing their conversation. "I guess I should be calling it a night myself. Thank you for all your help tonight in lining up some stories for me to listen to."

"It was my pleasure," Monica replied with a smile, "and don't forget about dinner tomorrow night. I think you will have quite an eye-opening experience." The two women said their goodbyes and went their separate ways into the night.

Chapter Ten - A Surprise for Rita

It was past 1 am when Rita walked through the door to her house. Although it had been many hours since she had crawled out of bed, she found herself a little too wired to sleep. Perhaps a glass of wine would relax her, she thought, and made her way into the kitchen. Two empty glasses sat on the counter, and she wondered who might have been keeping her husband company while she had been out trying to get information for her new book.

Picking them up, she noticed that one of the glasses had a lipstick stain around the rim. Then she caught a faint waft of perfume in the air. She thought perhaps that it was her imagination because of all the stories of infidelity that she had been listening to that evening.

She was surprised that her husband was not awake waiting for her since that was usually his habit. She poured herself a glass of wine took a small sip and then headed into the living room to relax for a few minutes before heading up to bed.

As she sat down in her favorite chair, she again caught a whiff of that same perfume, much stronger this time, so she knew that whoever it belonged to had been sitting in this very same chair.

Unable to stand the suspense, Rita drank the rest of her wine and headed up to her bedroom to confront her husband. He was lying in bed, and she could tell that he was only feigning to be asleep. "Ray, you can quit pretending now. I know that you are not asleep."

Ray did not move. He merely lay there with his eyes closed. Rita walked around the bed and yanked the bedding from his body. "We need to talk!" She demanded as his eyes flew open.

"And what would my dear wife like to talk about at this late hour? If you had wanted to talk, perhaps you should have been home hours ago."

"You knew where I was. And I know where you were as well. The question is, who was here with you?"

"Are you out of your mind, no one was here with me. I think all this research you are doing about cheating spouses has gone to your head."

"So I imagined the lipstick stains on the rim of one of the wine glasses on the counter? And the smell of perfume clinging to my favorite chair, am I imagining that as well?"

Ray hesitated to try to think of some logical explanation for the things his wife had just enumerated. And in fact, it was just that hesitation that convinced Rita that he was not telling the truth. Honest people do not have to take time before answering simple questions.

"So who is she, Ray?"

"Oh, for Christ's sake, Rita, so I forgot. Your sister stopped by looking for you. She stayed for a few minutes and had a glass of wine with me after I told her that you had gone out for the evening."

"So Charlene happened to stop by looking for me. I guess she must have figured that I would be here tonight since she just stopped by instead of calling. Is that the story, Ray?"

"It isn't a story for Christ's sake. It is the truth."

"There is one problem with your fabrication. I talked with Charlene, not 15 minutes before I left the house. She knew that I would be gone for the entire night. So if she was looking for something here, it sure as hell wasn't me."

Without another word, Rita left the bedroom and headed downstairs. Her first inclination was to sleep on the couch, but then another thought came into her mind. She had a hard time believing that her sister would betray her in her own house, but someone had sure been here, and from the lies that Ray was telling her that someone had been up to no good.

And then she remembered the playroom that they had set up in the basement. Not knowing what to expect, she opened the cellar door and slowly made her way down the steep steps. The smell of perfume was much stronger the further she descended, and she was positive that her husband had been entertaining a woman down here.

Turning on the light to the big room at the foot of the stairs, she stood for a minute and surveyed her surroundings. Clothesline still hung from the corners of the old metal desk, and an old floor mat was lying on the metal top.

On the floor next to that desk was a thick leather strap. She picked it up and immediately knew that it was specially designed as an implement for punishment. Ray had been so confident in his ability to pull the wool over her eyes that he had not even bothered to clean up after his night of debauchery.

She ran her hand over that mat and discovered that it was very stiff and would be uncomfortable to lie on, especially if you were naked and engaged in sexual activity. One thing was sure; if she did find the woman who had been tied down to that desk, she was sure her body would show evidence of the act.

With nothing left to accomplish, she got a blanket and pillow out of the hall closet and lay down on the sofa to get a little sleep.

It was a difficult night, and when the sun finally shone through the windows, it was a relief. She was just fixing coffee when she heard a loud pounding on the front door. She slipped on an old robe and went to see who was being so loud and so impatient at 7 am.

Much to her shock and dismay, when she looked through the peephole, a very angry brother-in-law stood on the other side. With a little trepidation, she pulled open the door, and Jason pushed past her, giving her a nudge to the side.

"Where is the bastard?" He demanded.

"Calm down and tell me what this is all about."

"What it is about is that I am going to beat your piece of shit husband to death with my bare hands."

"I know you are upset, but unless you calm down, I am going to have to call the police. You cannot just push your way into my home and threaten my husband, even if it is true that he might be a piece of shit."

She noticed tears start to form in the corner of his eyes, and she quickly put her arm around him and helped him to one of the kitchen chairs. She poured a cup of coffee and set it in front of him, not asking if he wanted anything in it. Perhaps the jolt of straight black coffee would settle him down enough for her to find out what was bothering him, although deep down inside, she was pretty sure she already knew. And if she found out her suspicions were true, Jason would be the least of Ray's worries.

Jason took a large gulp of the coffee before he realized just how hot it was. He threw his hand up in front of his face trying to keep the expectorate from flying all over the table. "Jesus Christ, that is hot." Then for the first time, he looked at the woman standing beside him. "Sorry about that, I guess I should test the water before jumping in with both feet."

"I should have warned you, but at least now you are calm enough so that you might be able to explain why you are here and what has you so upset with Raymond."

"I can show you better than tell you." He announced as he pulled his phone from his pocket and slid the arrow to unlock it. Quickly he pulled up his photos and passed the phone to Rita.

She gasped as she saw first the picture of her sister's black and blue back and then the raw blood-red picture of her breasts. "Oh my God, these are so horrible. What happened to my sister?"

"You need to ask that question of your sadistic bastard of a husband."

"I don't understand what you are implying." Rita insisted, although deep down, she knew exactly what had happened. She had found the evidence the night before; she just did not know who the victim had been. Now that she did know, she wanted to kill her husband every bit as much as Jason did.

"Where were you last night, Rita? Charlene told me that she was coming over here for a visit.

"I was out until after 1 in the morning. I was working on getting experience for a new book. And just so you understand, I told Charlene that I would not be home. So if she came over here, she was not looking for me. Surely you don't think that I had a hand in causing the damage I just saw in those photos?"

Just then, Ray came into the room and demanded to know why the two of them were making so much noise. Before the words had hardly left his mouth, Jason was in front of him, throwing a heavy punch to the side of his head. The shock and speed of the assault were so fast that Ray did not have a chance to defend himself. The blow was so powerful that it drove Ray to his knees and then prone on the floor. As he tried to get up, Jason delivered a devastating kick to his rib cage, and Rita heard what she figured was a cracking rib. Fearing for her husband's life, she grabbed hold of Jason and tried to pull him back away from the prone, helpless figure lying on the kitchen tile.

"For Christ's sake, Jason, get away from him. You are going to kill him."

"That is what I intend to do for what he did to my wife."

Rita stood her ground, having positioned herself between her husband and the husband of her sister. "I would suggest Raymond that you crawl out of this room before I turn Jason loose again. And don't even think about saying anything at this point, or I might give you a few bruises myself."

Ray wanted to open his mouth to try and defend himself, although he knew there was no defense. So he got to his knees and then painfully to his feet and exited the kitchen. He thought for a moment about calling the police, but then he remembered that he might share some culpability for what happened, and he did not want to open that can of worms.

Rita made sure that her husband had made it safely out of the kitchen and then turned back to her brother-in-law. "You seem pretty sure that Ray was responsible for the damage done to Charlene, why?"

"When she came home last night, she could barely walk. I asked her what was wrong, and she told me that she thought she had thrown her back out of place. So naturally, I tried to get her to allow me to massage it. She had a strange look on her face when she refused, and I knew right then there was more to the story than she was telling. So I told her I would draw her a nice warm bath so that her muscles could relax. She agreed, and I went upstairs and drew her a hot bath, and added some scented salts to the water. She would not start to undress until I left the room, so I pretended to be going downstairs to watch TV while she bathed. I gave her ample time to get undressed and into the tub before going back and trying the knob on the bathroom door. I found it locked, which confirmed my suspicions that something was badly out of whack. Fortunately, the lock is one that all you have to do is insert a small screwdriver into a hole and turn, and it comes right open. I guess she heard me coming, for she was trying to reach for a towel to cover up with when I walked into the room. She had her back towards me, and the first thing I noticed was that her back was covered in big black and blue stripes. It was obvious that if she had thrown her back out of place, it was trying to avoid being struck with some type of whip."

"And you believe that my husband would do that to his sister-in-law?"

"I didn't at first, but I had no idea who else might have done it. I told Charlene that I was going to call the police and then take her to the hospital. And that was before I saw what her front looked like. She immediately started begging me not to call the police or take her to the hospital. I already had my phone in my hand, and I snapped a few pictures to be used as evidence if it was needed for a court trial. She saw what I was doing and quickly turned around to avoid having her back photographed, and then I saw the damage to her breasts. At that point, I demanded an explanation, and when she refused, I pressed 911 on the keypad. When Charlene heard the emergency operator on the other end, she begged me to hang up, saying that she would tell me everything."

"I am waiting," Rita announced. "And what exactly did my sister tell you had transpired?"

"She told me that she had come over here looking for you and instead found Ray in an angry mood. It appeared he had been drinking, and when she tried to leave, he grabbed her shoved her down, and tied her hands behind her back. She thought that he had been waiting for such an opportunity because he had the rope already in one of his pockets."

"Okay, so continue. What happened next, according to Charlene?"

"She said that Ray then forced her to take off her clothes and began hitting her with some type of whip. And then he raped her."

"Really, and where did this supposed rape take place?" Rita already knew that her sister had been telling lies to her husband, but she needed to confirm her suspicions.

"She told me that he did it right on your sofa."

"Really, and how does that explain the abrasions on her breasts and front?"

"I don't know' at that point I was so angry that I wanted to kill the bastard. I still wanted to call the police, but she said she would be mortified if this came out in a trial, and so I figured the next best thing would be to get my revenge, and I came over here."

"Come with me. There is something that I want to show you." With that announcement, Rita headed to the cellar door.

Jason had no idea what was going on, but he figured the quickest way to find out would be to follow Rita and observe whatever she wanted to show him.

As they got to the foot of the stairs, he looked around for some reason he might be here, but all he saw was an old metal desk in the middle of the room. Rita, however, took his hand and led him to that desk. She pointed first to the stiff-bristled matt on the top and then to the ropes tied to each corner. And finally, she picked up the heavy taws from the floor and handed it to him.

"I think perhaps your wife has a little more explaining to do," Rita announced and then turned back towards the stairs.

As they reached the top of the stairs and again headed into the living room, Jason again took a look at the sofa. He shook his head and then again addressed Rita. "Okay, so I guess the reason behind that little trip downstairs was to make me doubt Charlene's story. So in your mind, what did happen, last night between my wife and your husband?"

"I am not completely sure, but one thing that I am positive about, and that is that Charlene did not get those abrasions on her tits and stomach by lying on my couch. Of course, that matt on the desk in the basement would certainly do the job. And the bruises on her back were more than likely caused by the taws that was laying on the floor beside it."

"So you're saying that Ray raped Charlene in your basement and that he tied her down to that harsh matt while he did it?"

"If that was what happened, then why did my sister lie to you and tell you the rape occurred in the living room on the sofa?"

"There you go again, answering a question with a question."

"At this stage in the game, I doubt that we should be asking questions of each other since neither of us was here at the time. I think it would be best if you have a long talk with your wife, and I have a long talk with my husband."

Chapter Eleven - Laura Pays a Visit to Her Father

After a restless night, Laura decided she needed to find out the truth, and the one person who could give her the necessary details would be her father. Normally she would be attending church services with her fiancé, but she had called and told him to go on without her.

She knew that her mother would be gone since she too always attended church on Sunday. In all the years of her being an adult, she had never seen her father accompany her mother to church, so she was quite certain she would have an opportunity for a talk without any interference.

When she arrived at her parent's house, she took out her key and quietly let herself in. She reasoned that if by some chance, her dad was sleeping, she did not want to disturb him. And unless her father was wandering around in the house naked, it should not be a problem with her just popping in unannounced. As she opened the front door, she could hear the vacuum running in the living room, so she headed in that direction.

She had to look twice at the scene taking place; before her eyes could process the information and send it to her brain. At first, she thought that perhaps her parents had hired a maid, but then she was positive that something else altogether was going on here. She was not sure she wanted to address this particular issue, now or anytime for that matter, and she tried to back out of the room and make her escape. But her father took that exact time to shut off the vacuum and look up and directly at her.

"Oh my God, Laura, what are you doing here this morning?" Her father's face was turning a bright shade of red. Of course, that might have been appropriate since it matched the shade of lipstick he was wearing.

"Daddy, I am so sorry. I should not have let myself in with my key, but I was afraid you might be sleeping, and I did not want to disturb you."

"Well, I guess the cat is out of the bag now, so you might as well stay. Would you like a cup of coffee?"

"I guess that would be okay if it isn't too much trouble."

"Why don't you have a seat, and I will bring it to you?"

Laura sat down in one of the big armchairs and put her head in her hands. This was not how she had pictured seeing her father this morning. She had come to talk with him about what her mother had told her the night before, but now this brought up a whole new range of questions to her mind.

Her father returned, carrying a silver tray with a pot of coffee, cream, and sugar on the side. "I wasn't sure how you took your coffee since you have left home, so I brought everything for you to fix your own." He took a cup for himself and settled into the chair across from her and daintily crossed his nylon-clad ankles. He took a small sip from his cup before speaking again.

"So I guess you must have wanted to talk with me about something. Perhaps you would like to fill me in."

"No, Dad, perhaps you should fill me in. Is this what you do for entertainment behind Mom's back? Does Mom even know about your crossdressing?"

"Your mother knows. She insists I dress this way anytime that we are not entertaining company. I don't know how she will feel about your finding out, but I guess it had to happen sometime."

"What do you mean she insists that you dress this way, exactly?"

"Your mother and I have a special kind of relationship. She found out several years ago that I enjoy being dominated by a strong, confident woman. Well, at first, it was just a game. I am not going to tell you about some of the kinky things we did, but eventually, her dominance moved out of the bedroom and into our total relationship.

On my days off, she would leave me a list of household chores for me to do, and then she would inspect what I had done when she returned that evening. Most of the time, she would commend me for a job well done and give me a small reward. Occasionally though, if I had not lived up to her expectations, she would have to discipline me. At first, that was accomplished by a bare-bottom spanking. But soon she discovered that I liked that type of punishment so she decided that perhaps humiliation would work better. So she started making me wear a pair of her panties under my clothes when I went to work. After a time, she added a garter belt and stockings. I hated that, as I was sure that someone in the office was going to find out. I begged her to allow me to go back to my male underclothing, and as a punishment for questioning her, she added a bra and told me that if I argued with her again, she would make sure I wore a thin enough shirt so that the bra would show through."

He hesitated at that point and took another dainty sip of his coffee.

"I don't understand, Dad, why would you put up with that?"

"Because I could see that it made her happy. Have you ever loved someone so much that you would do anything in the world just to see them smile?"

"I am not sure. I love Roger a lot, but I don't know if I would suffer this type of humiliation just to make him happy."

"If that is the case, then maybe you should rethink marrying the man. Until death do us part is a long time to live with someone that you are only lukewarm about."

"I would think that it would be a long time if you were miserable for the entire time." Laura tossed back.

"And what makes you think that I am miserable?"

"You just told me that Mom kept forcing you to wear more and more humiliating garments under your work clothes and how terrible that made you feel."

"I will not deny that I felt degraded thinking about how someone might discover my secret. But when I came home and saw your mother's beautiful face lit up with a huge smile because I had obeyed her, I felt wonderful. And this morning, when I prepared your Mother's breakfast and then helped her dress for church, I can honestly say that I have never loved her more. Her insisting that I dress as her maid only made the day more special."

"Hell, Dad, even I don't do housework wearing 5-inch heels. You have to be out of your mind."

"So, what was it that you wanted to talk to me about before you blundered upon me in a dress?"

"Truthfully, it was about something Mom said to me last night. Do you know where we went?"

"I think she said she was going to be taking you to something called "The Hot Wives Club." I am not sure exactly what it is, but I assume there were some pretty good-looking men there serving you drinks and food."

"Good looking is kind of an understatement. I have never seen so many muscles in one place before. I am going to be married in a few weeks, and I was drooling."

"Okay, so exactly what did your mother say that got you up in arms enough to come calling on a Sunday morning?"

"I am not going to say exactly what she said. I think there has been enough embarrassment to go around without that. But she alluded to the fact that she might be sleeping with other men and with your blessing."

"So who are you worried about embarrassing you or me?"

"You, I guess. Oh, hell, I don't know. Does it matter?"

"It only matters if you are afraid to ask me something for fear of my feelings. But the short answer to your question is yes, your mother does sleep with other men, and yes, I do sanction those actions. I learned a long time ago that I could not satisfy your mother in the bedroom even though I tried a lot of different methods to do so. So when she asked me about the possibility of her having an affair with a man she had met at work, I reluctantly at first gave her my blessing. But when she would come home and fill me in with all the details, it began to make me excited."

"Dear Lord, I simply cannot believe what you just said. So is your relationship what they call an open marriage?" The agitation in her father's voice was palpable as he spoke. Iris could feel the tension in the room, like a heavy fog that had settled over them. She took a deep breath, trying to steady herself before responding.

"You sound angry, daughter. Are you angry with your mother because you think she is abusing me? Or are you angry with me because I allow it? Or are you angry with God because he allows your mother to worship him?" His words were laced with pain and confusion, a raw vulnerability that Iris had rarely seen from him.

"Hell, I don't know maybe I am angry with myself because I don't understand any of this. How could I not have seen this when I came for visits?" Her frustration boiled over and she couldn't help but let it spill out.

"You did not see any of this because your mother did not think you were ready for it?" He seemed almost apologetic as if admitting his wife's actions were justified.

"And now suddenly she has decided to bring me into the fold, is that it?" Iris shook her head in disbelief, unable to fathom her mother's motives.

"You would have to ask her that, but since she shared a little of our lifestyle with you, I would assume she has her reasons. In any event, I think I hear her car pulling into the garage. I am sure she will be happy to have a heart-to-heart talk with you. I probably should be getting back to work." He stood up and left the room before Iris could respond.

Her father had hardly left the room when her mother entered through the connecting door to the garage. The click of her heels on the hardwood floor echoed through the room as she approached Iris.

"I saw your car out front. I missed you at church this morning. Roger mentioned that you would not be attending, but he did not explain why." Her tone was casual as if their conversation the night before had not happened.

"I needed to find out exactly what you were talking about last night at the club and so I decided I would pay a visit and have a talk with my father. Imagine my surprise when I used my key, let myself in, and came face to face with your maid." Iris couldn't hide the bitterness in her voice as she watched her mother's expression for any sign of remorse.

"Well, it was time that you found out about my maid. I hope she was busy when you came in." Her mother's words were cutting, like daggers aimed directly at Iris's heart.

"She was, vacuuming the living room carpet and in heels no less. I sure as hell wouldn't want to work for you." Iris could feel her anger rising.

"Would you like to stay for lunch? One of my lovers will be stopping by in just a little while. Perhaps you would like to meet him?" Her mother's smile was sickeningly sweet, but her eyes held a cruel glint.

"Yeah, well as lovely as that sounds, being present when you bring another man into the house to humiliate my father, I think I will pass." Iris couldn't stomach the thought of witnessing her mother's infidelities firsthand.

"Suit yourself." Her mother turned away and went to the kitchen counter. She picked up a small bell and rang it gently. Within moments, Iris's father appeared and curtsied to his wife.

"How may I be of service, Mistress?" His tone was polite and subservient, causing bile to rise in Iris's throat.

"Phil will be by in about 15 minutes. I wanted to make sure that you had time to change the sheets in the master bedroom and that the main bathroom is spotless. You know how particular Phil can be."

"Yes, Mistress, just as you commanded. I will prepare a light lunch for you and your guest. Will there be anything else?" Her father's words were measured and controlled as if he had rehearsed them countless times.

Chapter Twelve - Rita Confronts Her Sister

While Rita was in the basement with her brother-in-law, her husband had beaten a hasty retreat. Rita had intended to confront Ray and find out exactly what had happened the previous night, but now that would have to wait for another time.

As soon as Jason had left, Rita went to her bedroom and began to dress. Within a matter of minutes, she had donned a pair of jeans, a flannel shirt, and her favorite pair of athletic shoes. She ran a brush through her long auburn hair a few times, brushed her teeth, and headed for the door.

As she drove, she thought about what she would say to Charlene when she finally came face to face with her. She still could hardly believe that her sister had been in her house engaging in kinky sex with Ray while she was out working, but the evidence was almost overwhelming.

She expected to see Jason's car in the drive when she pulled up, but it was conspicuously missing. She figured that he must have gone somewhere to cool off after he had stopped by her place. She picked up a Sunday ad flyer off of the drive before walking to the door and ringing the bell. She waited a few seconds, and when Charlene did not answer the door, she began pounding loudly with the doorknocker.

"Jesus Christ, give me a minute, will you!" She heard her sister's voice ring out. And then the door was pulled violently inward. Charlene looked like she had been ridden hard and put away wet, and Rita almost felt sorry for her. But then she remembered why she had come here this morning, and she pushed her sister aside and stalked into the house.

"And good morning to you too, your highness." Charlene hissed. "What the hell do you mean by banging on my door this early on a Sunday morning?"

"I came over to find out what the hell you meant by fucking my husband in my basement last night. Now we can do this the civilized way over a cup of coffee, or I can beat the shit out of you and sit on your chest until you come clean. Which is it going to be?"

She was surprised when she looked into her sister's eyes and saw an almost explicit look of lust on her face. Then she remembered times when they were younger, and she had indeed done exactly what she had just suggested to Charlene. She had suspected at the time that her sister enjoyed being dominated by her, but she always covered it up well enough so that she could not be sure. But she had also always managed to do something else that caused her to have her face slapped to end up on her back. And then Charlene broke the tension.

"Let's try the coffee approach first. Perhaps you could beat the shit out of me a little later after I have had the time to wake up enough to enjoy it."

That was the last straw for Rita as she slapped her sister hard across the face. She reached out and grabbed the lapel of the robe her sister wore and tore it open, exposing Charlene's ample breasts. Charlene reached for the robe trying to pull it closed again, but Rita slapped her again this time directly across her mouth. "Leave it slut." Then reaching out, she grabbed one of Charlene's breasts and inspected the abraded skin. Pulling the robe off of her sister's shoulders, she spun the other woman around so that she could see what her back looked like. It was even uglier than the pictures that Jason had shown her.

"Is this what the attraction is with my Raymond? Do you come over so that he can abuse you while I am out for the evening?" She roughly spun her sister back around so she could look her in the eyes when she answered her questions.

To her surprise, Charlene had a look of amusement on her face. "Go ahead, hit me again. As you can see, I enjoy pain. But that isn't the only reason I visit your husband. Primarily I come over when you are gone so that he can plunge that huge cock of his into my cunt. Of course, if you were any kind of a real wife, he wouldn't need to find another woman to fuck."

Rita raised her hand to deliver another blow, but the look of lust on her sister's face stopped her. Instead, she grabbed her sister's hair and began pulling her into the kitchen. Charlene set her feet not because she wanted Rita to stop but because she enjoyed the feeling of having her hair pulled almost to the point of being yanked out by the roots. But Rita was determined, and soon Charlene found herself sitting on one of the kitchen chairs. She did not attempt to put her robe back on. She merely allowed it to drop off of her body and pool around her hips.

Rita ignored her as she went to the counter and rinsed out the coffee pot. She had visited enough times that she knew where everything was, and so she set about making a fresh pot of coffee. Flicking the switch, she waited to hear the first gurgles of hot water finding the grounds before turning back to her sister.

Charlene's look of defiance was almost more than Rita could take. "Charlene, I don't understand you. You sit there as if you haven't done anything wrong."

"Those words were never more true, sister. You don't understand me, but you do judge me. Just because I have needs that are different from yours doesn't mean that you can sit in judgment of me."

"Yes, well, I think you gave me that right when you started exercising those special needs of yours by using my husband to fulfill them."

"Oh, for Christ's sake, Rita, wake up and smell the coffee. If it had not been me, then Raymond would have found someone else to play with. I didn't force him to pick up that taws and use it on my back. And I sure as hell didn't force him to put that brutal matt under my tits while he fucked me. Those were his ideas, not mine."

Rita was surprised that she no longer felt anger towards her sister. As she looked into the face that once had been so sweet, she now felt pity for her. "Charlene, you need help. It is obvious that you are sick."

"Oh, so now just because you don't understand my needs, I am crazy. Is that it?"

"I did not say crazy. But you do need to see a professional therapist to help you understand this weird desire to have someone hurt you. One day someone is going to go too far, and you will end up in the hospital or worse."

"It's a little late for that big sister. I have been there, done that, and bought the t-shirt."

Rita looked at her sister with fresh concern in her eyes. "What do you mean by that, Charlene?"

"You, Mom, and Dad all thought that I was the clumsiest girl that ever lived. The time I said, I fell off my bike and broke my arm, or the times I would come home covered with bruises, and I told them some story about slipping in the woods and tumbling down a bank covered with rocks. Well, you will be amazed how many guys will beat a girl up especially if they find out that she will not squeal on them for it."

"Okay, now I guess I need to know how long has this been going on between you and my husband."

"Are you sure you want to know? You are not going to like the answer."

"I am sure that I am not going to like the answer, but don't you think I deserve one?"

"The first time was right after you came back from your honeymoon. You had given me a key so that I could come over and water your plants for you. Well, you came back a day early, if you recall and you did not tell me that you were coming. I guess you had gone to work to check on something, and Ray had stayed home. I didn't know anyone was in the house, so I let myself in with the key. I had watered the plants downstairs, and I proceeded up to water the ones in your bedroom. I heard a strange noise coming from the room, and so I opened the door real quiet-like.

My eyes widened in shock as I saw Ray sprawled out on the bed, completely naked except for one of your boots in his hand. His other hand was wrapped around his erect member, and he seemed lost in pleasure as he licked and sucked on the heel of the boot. I couldn't believe what I was witnessing and remained motionless, unable to process the scene before me. Suddenly, Ray looked up and caught my gaze, causing a deep red flush to spread across his embarrassed face. He stammered, trying to come up with a logical explanation for his actions - how does one explain to their sister-in-law why they are pleasuring themselves with their wife's footwear? The awkward silence hung heavy in the air as we both struggled to make sense of the situation.

I thought right then that this was too good to just let pass and so I started teasing him about being a pussy bootlicker. I threatened to tell you what I had found him doing, and before I could even react, he had come off that bed and grabbed me. He twisted my arm behind my back and told me that if I said one word about this to you he would hurt me badly. And then I told him that I would keep his secret if he did hurt me.

He grabbed the hair of my head and pulled it back hard, forcing me to look him in the eyes. 'Do you mean that?' He asked me. When I told him that I did, he sat on the edge of the bed and pulled me over his knees. He pulled up my dress pulled down my panties, and started to give me a spanking. He hit me over and over again until my ass was so bruised that I could not sit down the following day. I guess at some point, his hand must have started to get tired, and he stopped and started rubbing my ass cheeks. The next thing I knew, he was inserting a finger into my pussy. I was so unbelievably wet that he knew right away that his brutality had turned me on.

Without even asking, he pulled me off of his lap and threw me down on the bed. The next thing I knew, his cock was balls deep inside me, and I had the hardest orgasm I had ever experienced."

"My God, I can't believe what you just told me!" Rita exclaimed.

"Which part sis? The part about Raymond being a bootlicker or the part where I let him fuck me two weeks after your wedding? I suppose you want to know how many times he has fucked me since. Well, I can't tell you because I can't count that high. But I will tell you that I came over every time I knew you would be gone."

"I ought to beat the shit out of you myself, but I know that you would enjoy it, so I won't."

"You are a real sadistic bitch; you know that?" Charlene said with a smile. "I am sorry that it had to be your husband that I hooked up with. But once I found out how sadistic he was, I just couldn't help myself. Can I ask you a question?"

"Why not, after all this honesty we have been throwing around. What is it you want to know?"

"Well, I was just wondering if things between you and me would ever be okay again."

"Well, they might be except you have already told me that you can't quit seeing my husband. Maybe after I divorce the asshole, I could get around to forgiving you. Now for my question to you. What are you going to tell Jason? He already knows that the story you told him this morning is a pack of lies. He saw the desk in the basement. The matt was still on the top, and he knew that was what caused the abrasions to your tits."

"Don't worry about Jason. He is so pussy-whipped that I can always pull the wool over his eyes. I have convinced him to wear a chastity tube for me. That is where it is right now. The poor smuck is out shopping at adult novelty shops to find one."

"I just fucking don't believe you, Charlene. You get caught cheating on your husband, and he is the one who is going to wear the chastity device. Something is seriously fucked up with that man."

"I told you he is pussy whipped, and I intend to keep him that way."

With a look of unbelief on her face, Rita held her arms open, and Charlene took her up on the invitation. After they broke from their hug, Rita planted a little kiss on her sister's cheek. "I still think you should see a psychologist, but then I am the one trying to forgive you for fucking my husband. Maybe I should give Dr. Marks a call and arrange to have my head examined."

Chapter Thirteen - Rita Goes To Dinner

Rita was still confused as she drove home from her sister's house. How was it possible that she had never recognized the signs that must have been there ever since she had gotten married? Now, looking back, she could see that her husband's sexual appetite had waned, but she had just thought that was a common thing among married couples after a while. Now she realized that her husband's appetite had not diminished; he just desired a different kind of meal than what she had been cooking up.

Now she had to decide if it was worth it to change the recipe or just give up cooking for Raymond. She was relieved when she discovered that Raymond had not returned home by the time she had gotten dressed to go out for her dinner at Monica's house. She dressed kind of conservatively in a black knee-length skirt, a cream-colored satin blouse, and a pair of medium heels.

She had been so busy trying to figure out her own life that she arrived about a half-hour later than when she had expected. "Sorry I am late," She announced as Monica opened the door and invited her in.

"That is perfectly all right. Dinner won't be ready for another hour or so anyway. I just thought we could have a chat while we waited. Would you like something to drink before dinner?"

"Sure anything you have as long as it has a kick to it."

"Roy makes a pretty good margarita if you are into tequila."

"Sounds good to me."

As Rita watched, Monica picked up a small bell from the stand beside her chair and began to ring it. Rita let out a small chuckle causing Monica to cock one eyebrow in the form of a question."

"Sorry about that. It just seems like that is something that one sees in a movie and not in real life."

Before Monica could answer, her husband came into the room. He was dressed as the perfect French Maid would complete with his cap and apron both with lace trim. On his feet was a pair of extremely high-heeled shoes. Monica could not help but stare at them when she saw that the straps across the top of his feet were locked in place with two small padlocks.

"Slave get Rita and me a picture of margaritas and make sure that the glasses are properly prepared with some salt around the rims. And remember to put a wedge of lime on as well."

"Yes, Mistress." And before he turned to leave the room, he gave a perfect little curtsy to both ladies.

"Oh, my God, he is so adorable in that outfit. Isn't he just mortified to be seen wearing it with company present, though?"

"He used to be, but he got over the embarrassment a long time ago. And I insist that he wears a maid's uniform any time he is here in the house. Occasionally I even loan him out to some of the other ladies from the club, and once in a while, I even send him over to my lover's house to clean and do laundry. Of course, he has to dress properly on those occasions as well."

"I find it hard to believe that a man would clean house for his wife's lovers. How long has this been going on, if you don't mind me asking?"

"Oh, I discovered early on in my marriage that Roy was submissive to me. We have been married for 22 years now, so I guess he has been my slave for 21 of those years. I guess it took me another three years before I had him well enough trained that he willingly agreed to allow me to take lovers while he remained chaste."

"You said you discovered early on that he was submissive to you. How did you find that out?"

"It was little things at first. I would catch him staring at my feet. I figured he had a foot fetish, and I thought I would take advantage of it by demanding that he give me foot massages. He willingly agreed, and about the third night, I jokingly suggested that he should be on his knees to do the job properly. Much to my surprise and delight, he did not even question it. He just dropped to his knees and started massaging my feet as if it were the most natural thing in the world. So the next night I didn't even have to tell him. And when he got on his knees, I raised one foot to his lips and demanded that he kiss it. When he did, I repeated the process with my other foot.

So the next night, when he dropped to his knees in front of me, he simply picked up each of my bare feet and began kissing them. I figured I wanted to see how far I could push this newfound power, so I told him I wanted him to suck on my toes. He did that so greedily that I ordered him to lick the soles of my feet clean. It seemed to be a natural progression to have him greet me on his knees when I would enter the house. I then demanded that he begin kissing my footwear before he would take them off of me."

Rita let out a little gasp when Monica started to tell her about making Roy lick her shoes.

"Dear, what is the matter? Did I say something to upset you?" Monica asked.

"No, it is just that when you said that about having him lick your shoes, it reminded me of something my sister told me earlier today. I know this is your story, but I need to share this with someone before I burst."

"Please, I would love to hear whatever it is that you want to tell me."

So Rita began to tell Monica about what had happened between Raymond and her sister the night before. She went into great detail about the bruises on Charlene's back, the abrasions on her front, and how she had confronted her. When she finally got to the part about how the affair had started, and she told Monica about Raymond being caught with one of her high-heeled boots in his mouth, Monica interrupted the story.

"You do realize what his licking your boots means, don't you?"

"I thought it meant that he liked the taste of dirty leather until I heard your story about Roy licking your shoes."

"It means that he fantasizes about being dominated by you. I know that you are angry with him right now and are probably thinking of kicking his ass to the curb, but this could be the start of something great for you. Just imagine having your own maid and housekeeper. Imagine never having to wash a dish clean a toilet or vacuum a carpet again. Imagine having your clothes properly laundered and ironed for you. And better yet, imagine having Raymond bathe you and get you ready so that you can go out on a date with another man while he stays home and makes sure that everything you desire is done while you are gone."

Just then, Roy returned with an ice-cold picture of drinks and two salted glasses. He set the tray on the table and turned to his wife. "Will there be anything else before I serve dinner, Mistress?"

"No slave, but aren't you forgetting your manners?"

"Many pardons, Mistress. I did not know if you expected the usual greeting from a guest in the house or not. I thought I should err on the part of caution."

"My guest knows all about your service to me, slave. Now greet her properly."

"Yes, Mistress." He replied as he sunk to his knees in front of the women. Crawling first to Rita, he bent his head and kissed both of her shoes. He then crawled back to his wife and repeated the process on her boots. He did not get back to his feet until he was almost to the doorway. Only then did he rise, give each woman a little curtsy before exiting.

"God, I just love that. I am so pissed at Ray that I would like to force him to kiss my feet in front of everyone he knows. And then since he enjoys giving pain the way he does, I would like to see how he would enjoy being on the receiving end for a change."

Just then, Roy came back into the room, freshened their drinks, and announced that dinner would be served in five minutes. They made their way to the table, and Roy helped each of them to their seats. Rita noticed that there were only two place settings, and she asked if Roy would be joining them.

"Heavens no, the slave does not eat at the table of his Mistress. Roy will eat in the kitchen once we have finished, and he has cleared and cleaned the dishes."

The meal was divine, the service impeccable, and the wine heady. Rita was feeling very relaxed and happy as she watched Roy clear the last of the dishes away from the table. He topped off both women's wine glasses before making his final exit.

"Would you like to take your wine into the living room where you can better relax, dear?" Monica asked her.

Rita acknowledged that she would enjoy that and as they sat down in the plush chairs, she again thought of why she was there and proposed one more question. "I am curious about how your first extramarital affair began."

"What would you like to know?"

"Everything. How long had you been married, why you decided to do it, and how Roy reacted."

"Well, the first time it happened, Roy did not know about it. At least he didn't know when it first began. Eventually, I told him, and he didn't take it too well. But I am getting ahead of myself. I had always been sexually active, even long before I graduated from high school. And in college, I was pretty much a slut. I loved to fuck, and I loved the variety. I thought that I could just shut that off when I got married, and maybe I could have if Roy had been better endowed. But I bought the old line that size does not matter and boy is that a load of crap. Perhaps the length isn't quite so important, but the girth is what makes my pussy purr.

So I tried hard for the first year trying to reconcile the fact that Roy could not satisfy me with the fact that I was supposed to keep myself only to him. An epic battle of good and evil was waging, and the battlefield was my cunt. Pardon my language."

"Oh please, my readers love a little color in the language. And the ones that would complain about the word cunt should not be reading what I write to begin with."

Monica laughed a little before continuing. "Well, one night, Roy had a little too much to drink, but he thought we should have sex, regardless. Even at his best, he couldn't last very long, but when he was two sheets to the wind, he was worthless. And so the next few minutes went something like this.

"Please, Roy, slow down. Please slow down; I am not ready yet. Damn you, I said slow down," I raged.

But Roy had already started to orgasm, and he had no control over his body at that point. With one deep thrust, he released a stream of white-hot cum into my body. Exhausted, he allowed his weight to settle on top of me as he struggled to get his breath.

"Get off of me, you son of a bitch," I demanded. "Get off now."

Never had he seen his wife this angry or heard her use such language directed at anyone, no less him. "Honey, I am sorry. I just could not help myself. I promise I will make it up to you next time."

"There will not be a next time. I have had it with your sad excuse for an attempt at sex. All you think about is your pleasure. I should have known something was wrong when you wanted to wait until we were married to have sex with me. If I had seen your pathetic excuse for a cock beforehand, I would never have married you. Now get the fuck out of this bed and leave me alone."

"Wow, that must have been devastating to Roy. What happened next?"

"I didn't speak to him for a couple of days after that, but finally, when he came begging on his knees, I decided to not only speak to him but to lay down the law.

Roy, I think that it is time we made some changes in our marriage. The other night was the last straw for me when it came to not being satisfied in the sex department. I should have told you a long time before this that you simply do not satisfy me in bed. I don't know whether it is your chronic masturbating or not, but I have decided that you are not going to be playing with your little Willy anymore.

Of course, he tried to reason with me saying that a man needed release, and if he could not get it from his wife, then he had to get it by hand. I think he had thought about saying he had to get it from someone else, but the look in my eye told him that would be an unwise decision.

That was the first time that I ever slapped him across his face. Well, he turned meek as a church mouse and dropped down and kissed the tops of my shoes immediately. And I knew that I had him right where I wanted. I took him to the computer and opened the browser to a website about male chastity. I showed him what I wanted him to buy and instructed him to find someplace local where he could be fitted. I told him that I did not want the device to stop him from attaining an erection altogether, but I wanted it to stop him from ejaculating once he was hard. I figured that way I could use his ardor to get more of the things I desired. I figured that I would only keep him locked up for a short time and then try to have sex with him again after he had abstained for a while.

A couple of nights later, he brought the thing home with him after work. He came in and showed it to me, and I immediately had to see how it worked. So I ordered him to the bedroom and had him strip out of his clothes. I looked at the tube and then back at his fully erect penis and knew that the first was not going on the second until all of that swelling went down. I reasoned that I could relent and allow him to masturbate one last time, but I did not want that to happen. He suggested that we might apply some ice directly to the glans. He had read somewhere that was what a lot of women used to get an erection to go down so that they could encase their men's penis in chastity. I laughed, thinking how long that might take, and I took a ruler off of my vanity and gave him a hard smack to the glans. He screamed and tried to cover up, but another slap across his face got him to drop his hands. I kept hitting him with the ruler until he was as soft as the day he was born. Then I put the device on him and put the key away in a safe place.

I didn't mention it for about a week, and then he came begging me to take his little wiener out of the tube so he could get some relief. His begging turned me on, and so I told him if he did a really good job of licking me to orgasm, I might consider it.

He was on his knees in a flash, pulling my panties down and pulling my legs apart. I grabbed him by his hair and forced him to crawl as I backed slowly towards the bed. I lay back on the mattress with my legs hanging off the edge. When he got into position, I put my legs on either side of his face and pulled him to what was a now dripping snatch.

I was getting into dominance as I ground his face back and forth against me. I could hear him begging me for something, but I just closed my legs a little bit harder around his face to cut out the sound. I felt him beginning to thrash hard in an attempt to escape, and I finally relented and opened my legs.

'I couldn't breathe.' He complained.

Then make sure you keep your tongue moving, and your nose against my clit or I will smother you. Well, he worked harder than he had ever in the past, and I had a massive orgasm while his mouth was still working on the folds of my cunt.

When I finally settled down and allowed him to get back to his feet, I looked at his face and was happy to see that it was covered with my juices. I told him to leave it that way and that I would tell him when it was time to wash it off. A few hours later, I laughed at him when I saw those juices had dried onto his face. Of course, he had licked everything off of his lips with his tongue."

Rita was looking at her old friend and just began shaking her head from side to side.

"What?" Monica demanded. "You said you wanted to hear the whole story."

"Yes, but I am shocked. How long have we known each other? How could I have not seen this side of you?"

"You're shocked? How do you think I felt? One day I am this sweet, demure, unassuming woman who had never done anything wrong in her entire life, and then the next, I am some maniacal monster who not only enjoys abusing her husband but gets off sexually while she is doing it."

After a brief respite to allow the laughter to clear their systems, Monica resumed her story. "So even though he had done a splendid job with his tongue, I refused to release him from his cage. Every night he would come to me and beg to be released, and every night I would hold the carrot in front of his nose, telling him that I might if he brought me to an orgasm with his tongue. And for a time, I was quite happy with just having him give me oral ministrations. But after a while, I needed a cock stuffed deep inside me. Oh, I tried vibrators and dildos, but nothing takes the place of a real cock.

I was almost to the point where I thought about releasing Roy and having him give it another go. But about that time my boss asked me to go with him to a conference. He said it was strictly business, so I agreed.

The first night after all the meetings was over; everyone went down to the bar to have a few drinks and unwind. We had a light meal at the bar as well and after we ate the band started to play some old, slow songs. My boss asked me if I would like to dance with him, and I readily accepted. I was a little surprised when he took me into his arms that one of his hands ended up on my ass instead of my waist. He kept pulling me tighter and tighter into his embrace, and soon I could feel his cock pressing against me through our clothes. It felt enormous, and I was not sure if it was real or if he had stuck a banana down his shorts.

When the music stopped, he did not release me but just held me there waiting for another song to start. Once again, I was swaying against something long and hard, and I began salivating just thinking about having that something shoved inside of me.

When we finally went back to the bar, I pulled my stool a little closer to him and dropped my hand down to rest on the inside of his thigh. He reached down and immediately positioned it right on top of his cock. I gave it a little squeeze, and he loudly called for the check. The next thing I knew, we were in the elevator, and I was back in his arms only now my mouth was locked onto his, and I was exploring with my tongue seeing what I could find in there. He tasted so good, a mixture of bourbon and man. There was even a hint of tobacco from some time earlier in the evening. Our tongues danced together the same way our bodies had, and my panties were so wet that I was afraid that he could smell my sex.

But then his hand was under my dress, and his fingers were exploring, and my secret was not so secret anymore. He said, 'God, you're wet. I would like to fuck you right here in the elevator. I wanted him to as well, but right then it stopped, and a couple of other guys entered the car. They stared at me, and I knew that they had figured out what was going on.

I was more surprised when Marvin smiled at them and then went back to kissing me and fingering my cunt right in front of them. I was almost surprised when he didn't invite them to join us in his room, but I guess the first time he wanted me all to himself. I was so hot that if he had suggested I take three cocks that evening, I would have gladly accepted.

As we entered the room, he did not even bother to take my clothes off. He just pushed me down on the bed, pulled my panties to one side, and drove his cock straight into my hot wet snatch. I exploded with a mammoth orgasm before he had taken three strokes, and then I came again and again before he finally released his white-hot cum deep inside me. I know that was a stupid thing letting him fuck me without a condom, but when all your mind can concentrate on is cock things like that happen.

Of course, I was on the pill, so all I had to worry about was STDs."

By the time Monica had gotten to that point in her story, Rita was completely aroused. She knew that Monica could smell her sex because she could smell it herself. She caught Monica staring at her lap, and her face turned a couple of shades pinker.

"You are breathing a little heavy, my dear, and your face is a little flushed. Did my story upset you in some way?"

"You know damn well what your story did to me. The entire room smells like hot wet pussy, and it is coming from between my legs. Damn, right now, I wish there was a man present. I would jump his bones right here in front of you. Unfortunately, unless you have someone hidden away that I don't know about, the only male present is your husband, and you have already told me how worthless he is between the sheets."

"And just why does it have to be a male, dear? Have you ever thought of being with a woman? Didn't you ever experiment with girl-on-girl action when you were in college?"

Rita looked at her friend and then sadly shook her head. "I am not sure that I am ready to go that route yet. And it is getting late; I think for both our sakes I should be heading home. Would you tell Roy how much I appreciated his help and attention this evening?"

"You can tell him yourself, dear. I know he would like to say goodnight properly to you."

Monica picked up her little bell and gave it a gentle shake. Roy entered the room, almost as if he was poised and waiting to do so.

"Rita will be leaving now, slave. Walk her to her car and make sure she gets in safely."

"Yes, Mistress." He then turned to Rita. "Whenever you are ready, Mistress." And he offered her his arm.

She handed her keys to Roy and stood back as he opened her door for her. She watched his eyes as she slid in behind the wheel and marveled that he never once looked down to catch a glimpse of her thigh as her skirt slid up her legs. When she was situated, he closed the door but stood back, waiting to make sure her car started, and she was on her way. She lowered the driver's side window and addressed him. "Roy, is it all right if I ask you a question?"

"Of course, Mistress. What would you like to know?"

"I was just wondering, are you happy?"

Roy's lips curved upward in a smile. No, that was an understatement, his entire face lit up, "Do you mean am I happy being my wife's slave? I cannot think of another thing in this world that I would like more. You see, I loved her very much when we got married, but once I discovered how dominant she could be, I fell even more in love with her. There is not one thing that my wonderful Mistress could ask of me that I would hesitate to do."

"But isn't it hard seeing her make love to other men?"

"It was at first. I got so jealous that I almost flew into a rage the first time she brought a man home to our bed. But once I saw and heard how much that man was giving her pleasure, while it still hurt, I had to accept the fact that I had no real choice in the matter. Monica made it plain to me that I was not able to please her in bed, and she was not going to live a celibate life. Now I just accept the fact that other men will be coming by from time to time to pleasure Monica. I also accept the fact that while they are in our home, they are my Masters to be obeyed in the same way I would obey Monica. Does that answer your question?"

"It brings more questions to mind, but I am afraid I need to be heading home. Thank you so much for all your attention."

"No thanks required, Mistress. When you are in Monica's home, I am your servant. Drive safe."

She started the car drove around the oval driveway and headed back towards the street. Several times she checked her rearview mirror and noticed that Roy was still standing there watching her drive off.

Chapter Fourteen - Rita Confronts Ray

It was two days later that Ray finally got up the nerve to return to his house. He had thought long and hard about what he would tell Rita when she confronted him. And he did not doubt that she would bring the matter to the forefront of their conversation.

Having no better option, he thought that the best course of action was one that he was extremely familiar with, he would lie.

He did not see his wife's car in the drive, and he breathed a little sigh of relief as he entered the house. He needed a quick shave and shower, so he headed up to his room and the master bath that was attached to it. He entered the bedroom and noticed that everything was neat and tidy, so he did not know if Rita had not slept there or if she had simply made up the bed after she had. There was one thing out of place, however, and that was a pair of Rita's knee-high leather boots sitting out in plain view.

A niggling of suspicion entered his mind when he saw them, but he quickly put the thought out of his mind as an old lust took over. As if they were magnetic and he was a piece of iron, he was drawn to those boots.

He felt his cock begin to lengthen and thicken as he picked up both boots and carried them to the bed. He held first the left one to his nose and took a long whiff from inside the boot and then did the same with the right one. He began to feel a little light-headed much the way a smoker would having his first cigarette of the day. Almost without realizing what he was doing, he discarded first his shirt and then his pants. He was soon completely naked, and he rubbed the leather of her boots against his rock-hard member, uttering a groan of pleasure as he did so. Now, if he only had a pair of her panties, everything would be perfect.

It was extremely difficult for him to forego his pleasure, but he sacrificed it for the moment for what he knew would be even more satisfying. Opening the closet door, he opened the top of the laundry hamper and sought through the layers of clothes until he found the treasure he was looking for, a pair of Rita's used panties. He turned them inside out and spread the material until he could see the crotch that had recently rested firmly against his wife, slightly moist pussy.

He quickly put them against his nose and drew in the heavenly aroma of his wife's sex. Sticking out his tongue, he also tasted what was left on the material, and he longed for the real thing. He thought about sinking to his knees in front of his wife and sticking his tongue between the folds of her cunt, lapping every drop of wonderful slick moisture that he could find. Oh, if she only knew how he worshipped at her altar.

A drop of precum appeared from the slit on the head of his cock, and he milked it off onto one of Rita's boots. He smeared it as far as it would go onto boot toe and then went back and began squeezing from the base of his cock to the tip until another even larger glistening glob appeared. This one went onto the toe of her other boot. Using the tip of his cock this time instead of his finger, he spread the sticky fluid as far as it would go.

Wrapping the used panties around his cock, he began stroking it with his right hand as he brought one of the boots to his lips with his left. He imagined his wife ordering him to lick the leather clean, and his cock grew almost to the bursting point. He wanted it to last a long time, so when he felt his balls beginning to contract, he took his hand away from the shaft until the quivering slowed down. He concentrated on the boots and had the cum completely licked clean.

He tentatively ran his tongue along the sole of the boot, but he did not like the taste of that nearly as much as he did the leather of the uppers. He imagined that his wife was forcing him to suck her lover's cock, and he pulled the boot heel deep in his mouth and began sucking on it as if it were a phallus. Again he had a hold of the satin-wrapped cock, and he could no longer hold back. The pleasure was too great, and his balls were constricting. He tightened his legs and ass muscles, and within a few more seconds, a large spurt of cum came flying out of the tip. He quickly grabbed one of her boots, and the second spurt landed on the shaft of the boot, making a sticky mess. Again his balls pumped more white-hot goop up and out of the tip, this time landing on the other boot.

When his balls were completely drained, and his muscles began to relax, he picked up the boots and looked at the mess he had caused. While he was hard and getting ready to ejaculate, he fantasized about how wonderful it would be to be forced to lick up his cum and ingest it. But now that his balls were empty, the thought was completely revolting to him. He quickly laid the boots on top of the coverlet, making sure that the sticky side was up. He hurried into the bathroom and unrolled a large wad of toilet paper and came back to the bed. He used the paper to wipe up as much of the cum as he could only to have it begin to shred, leaving small bits of paper stuck to the boots.

His conscience was working overtime, now realizing that he stood a very good chance of being caught unless he could find a better way of cleaning those boots. And then his worst nightmare came in the form of him hearing a car in the drive. He was out of time, and all he could do was rush back to the closet and deposit those panties into the hamper. Grabbing the boots, he also shoved them into the closet and pushed them back behind some other shoes and boots that were neatly lined up on the carpet.

He then rushed into the bathroom and locked the door. He knew he needed to shave, but he didn't think he had the time, so He turned on the water in the shower and stepped in before he had even checked the temperature. He let out a little scream of pain as the much too hot water hit his chest, stomach, and legs. Stepping back quickly, he turned the faucet to a colder setting only to have turned it too far, and now cold water jetted out at him. Letting out another audible curse, he finally got the water temperature adjusted to a reasonably comfortable setting when he heard his wife call his name.

"Raymond, are you all right in there? I thought I heard you cry out."

"No, Rita, I am fine. I am just taking a shower. I will be out in a moment."

"Take your time, dear; I am just going to get dressed to go out tonight. By the way, have you seen the pair of boots I am going to wear, you know the black leather knee-high boots? I could have sworn that I left them here by the closet door. I must be losing my mind."

Rita smiled to herself as she planted that thought into the mind of her husband. She looked up at the bookshelf across from the bed and noticed that the camera light was blinking, indicating that it was on and operational. She could still hear the sound of water running in the shower, so she used the opportunity to retrieve the disc from the video camera. She went downstairs and popped it into her computer and turned it on. The tableau that she saw both shocked and pleased her. Raymond was going to have some explaining to do, but first, she was going to have some fun with him.

When she returned to the bedroom, Raymond was out of the shower, and he had a towel wrapped around his waist. She looked at his face and saw that he was sprouting at least two days of whiskers and shook her head. "Ray, have you decided to grow a beard?" She asked him.

"No, I guess I just didn't remember to shave."

"Are you becoming forgetful? Perhaps I should call and get an appointment with our doctor for you. I wouldn't want senility to begin to set in at such a young age."

"Jesus, Rita, let it go, haven't you ever forgotten something?"

"Yes, as a matter of fact, I have. I have forgotten where I put my black boots. You haven't seen them have you?"

"No, but you have a whole closet full of boots and shoes. What difference does it make which pair you wear today? Here let me get a pair for you. Sit on the bed, and I will help you put them on."

He immediately went to the closet and pulled out a pair of ankle-high black leather boots that he found particularly attractive on his wife. He brought them back to the bed and dropped down on his knees in front of her. Grabbing one foot, he pulled off the shoe she was wearing and began to put the boot on in its place. Rita tightened her foot, making it more difficult for him to get the boot on. Ray kept working on his task, but he was not having a lot of success since Rita was working against him.

"Raymond, what do you think you are doing?" Rita finally spoke. "I haven't even picked out what I am going to wear, and I need to take a bath and do my hair before I get dressed."

Ray breathed a sigh of relief because now he saw an opportunity to clean up the mess he had created while his wife was out of sight in the bathroom. "Would you like me to draw your bath for you?" He asked.

"No, Raymond. I am sure you have things to do. And just so you don't think that I have lost my mind, we still have something to talk about, so don't even think about leaving this house until we have ironed out some things."

"Oh, Christ. Do we have to dredge up the nonsense from the other day? Can't we just let bygones be bygones?"

"I am afraid not, but right now, I need to take that bath. I will see you downstairs in about an hour."

Rita loved the look of alarm on her husband's face. If only he knew how much more devastated he was going to be in an hour or so. As he left the bedroom, she calmly walked into the closet and looked in the only place he would have had time to hide her boots. She pulled them out and snapped a few pictures of the mess on both shafts before setting them back in place. With a big smile on her face, she slipped into the bathroom and began drawing a tub of water.

As soon as Ray was sure that his wife would be in the bathroom for a while, he came back upstairs with a towel he had wet in the kitchen sink. He entered the closet closed the door behind him, and quickly pulled the boots from their hiding place. Not knowing how much time he had, he hastened to clean all the cum that was left on the shafts of both boots. Satisfied that he had destroyed all the evidence, he set the boots beside the others on the front row. He chuckled a little to himself as he made his escape thinking how close he had come to a disaster.

"It is better to be lucky than good." He thought.

He was just fixing a light lunch for the two of them when Rita came downstairs and into the kitchen. She was wearing a thick terry robe, which surprised him as he was sure that she would have gotten dressed by now. "I thought you were going to get dressed to go out?"

"I am, but I have plenty of time. I thought we could have lunch and then that little talk I mentioned. I see you have some sandwiches prepared, how about a cup of coffee to go with them?"

They ate in relative silence; neither one broaching the elephant in the room. Finally, when they had eaten, and the table cleared, Rita spoke.

"I went over and had a little talk with Charlene the other day after Jason left here. By the way, how are your ribs? Have they healed up some?"

"My ribs are fine. So let's get the interrogation over with. What did your slut of a sister tell you?"

"So now my sister is a slut? And what makes you say a thing like that?"

"Well, isn't it obvious? She is always coming on to me every time you turn your back. I'll bet she has fucked half the men in town."

" I didn't know that you harbored so much ill will towards Charlene. So I suppose you have never had any thoughts that you might like to get into her pants?"

"Hell, no. She is so not my type."

"And what type would that be, Ray?"

He knew that he had to be careful. It would be so easy to fall into a trap the way his wife was wording her questions. He was surprised that she was remaining so calm through this whole ordeal, especially after hearing the accusations that Jason had tossed out a few days previously.

"You know, Rita, you are the only woman for me. So I guess you would be my type."

"Ah, that is so sweet. I find it funny though that you haven't been very attentive to me lately, though. I can't remember the last time we had sex together, do you?"

Now he could see her trap was beginning to spring shut, and he had to find a way to get out from between the jaws. "Honey, you know how busy we both have been. You are always away getting information for your books, and I am working a lot of overtime. I guess we will just have to make time for each other's needs."

"Hmm, I guess that makes sense. Hey, I have an idea why don't we have a little afternoon tryst today? We are both here now." Rita walked over and began unbuttoning Ray's shirt. Pulling it off his shoulders, she then reached for his belt. Now terror began to sink into the very core of Ray's being. He knew that his cock should be responding, but after the workout, he had given it earlier and the guilty conscience he was experiencing, it just would not rise to the occasion. He instantly knew that if he did not stop this, he would have to explain the flaccid condition of his cock, so he took Rita's hands as gently as possible away from his belt.

"What's the matter, lover? I thought you would be raring to go since it has been God knows when since your little member has had any action." She again reached for his belt, and this time he roughly shoved her hands away.

"God damn it, Rita, I said no. Why do you have to be so damned, insistent? Once you get an idea in your head, you just have to push it to a conclusion.

"Well, perhaps I am not your type, after all. Why don't we get back to the main topic of conversation since it is obvious that you don't want to fuck? You were telling me that you have never even thought of having sex with my sister. So how do you explain the abrasions on her tits and the black and blue marks on her back? She told me that you did that to her. Why do you think she would say such a thing if it wasn't true?"

"Your sister is a lying bitch. She is just trying to cover her ass. She probably snuck out with some guy, and he took advantage of her masochism and beat her up."

"So now my sister is a masochist? Tell me, Ray, how would you know that?"

Ray knew that Rita should be much madder than she seemed to be, and her calm demeanor was affecting him. He could feel a small droplet of sweat beginning to form under his armpits, and he prayed that his deodorant would mask the smell of his fear.

"I don't know; I guess I just assumed by the way she acts around me."

"Hmm, I can't see you getting that type of a feeling just from being around her. Did she ever say something that might have led you to believe she enjoys pain?"

I have never been alone with her long enough to find out anything she likes. Can we just drop this whole line of questioning, please?"

"You seem to be getting a little wound up, Ray. Does talking about Charlene's sexual tastes bother you that much?"

"No, what bothers me is that you seem to be accusing me of something that I haven't done."

"So then when she was over here the other night, you didn't take her down into our basement? You didn't put a course mat on top of the desk and then tie her face down? You didn't fuck her while you took a taws and beat her shoulders until they turned black and blue?"

"For Christ's sake, no. Why would you even think such a thing?"

"Well, for one reason, she told me that was what happened."

Ray opened his mouth to again call Charlene a liar, but Rita leaned forward and put a finger against his lips as a sign for him to be quiet.

"I know that you are going to try to deny it, but you see all the evidence supports her story. For instance, if it did not happen, then how she would know about the desk in the basement that she says you tied her to? And how would she know about the mat she says you placed on top of that desk? And how would she know about the taws that I found lying beside that same desk? You have to become better at covering up your indiscretions."

Ray wanted to say something in his defense, but he could not form the correct words. He knew that if this was a murder trial with him as a defendant he would get the death penalty. No juror in the world would believe his lame story after being confronted with this massive pile of proof.

"Okay, maybe I did have a little fling with the cunt. Can you blame me when she came over here, begging me to fuck her? I am only human, you know?"

Again Ray was sure that now Rita would go berserk, but again she remained calm. "Now that we have gotten that out in the open, why don't you tell me the whole truth? How long have these little sexual episodes been going on?"

Ray thought a little too long before he answered, and Rita realized immediately that he was trying to come up with a convincing story.

"It was just that once, I swear to you."

"That is so strange. I wonder why Rita would tell me that this has been going on since the day we came back from our honeymoon. She could have gotten off much easier by simply telling me that it only happened once as you did. However, she insists that you have been fucking her every time I leave the house for years. She says that you inform her when I tell you that I am going out, and then she comes over for a little pleasure and pain."

"I have already told you that she lies."

"Yes, you have mentioned that. But one of the lies you insisted that she told me you have now admitted was the truth. It makes me wonder if one thing wasn't a lie; perhaps another thing might be true as well. Do you know what she told me you were doing the first time she came over before you had sex with her?"

Ray knew all too well what Charlene had told his wife. And now he was terrified that he might be caught up in another huge untruth.

"No, but I am sure you are going to tell me. So get it over with. I am sure it is a doozy. As a matter of fact, it is a little bizarre. I was shocked, and I thought there was no way in hell that my man would be caught masturbating with one hand while he used his other to hold one of my dirty boots to his mouth to lick it clean."

"Dear God, certainly you don't believe such a thing do you?"

"Which part? The part where you were caught masturbating or the part where you were licking the dirt off of my boots?"

"Either one!" Ray exclaimed.

"Oh, so then you don't ever masturbate? Is that your story?"

"Well, I am not going to try and convince you of that. Everyone masturbates occasionally. I bet even you rub the nub now and then."

"Well, I guess I can admit to that. I wanted to rub the nub as you put it while listening to Monica tell me how she had turned Roy into her slave. God, that is so hot thinking about actually owning a man. Having him do all the housework while you relax. Having him greet you when you walk into the house by having him drop to his knees and kiss your feet. Have you ever thought about being my slave, Ray?"

"Of course not, that would be sick. Why would you even ask me such a thing?"

"Well, it is just that when I told Monica about what Charlene had said about catching you licking my boots, she told me that was a classic sign of someone who wanted to be dominated. Do you think that bootlickers want to be dominated, Ray?"

"How in hell would I know?"

"I guess you wouldn't if you weren't a bootlicker? But then why do you suppose that Charlene insisted she had caught you licking my boots? Have you ever licked my boots, Ray?"

"Of course not, I have already told you no."

"So I suppose you wouldn't want to make a little bet, would you? If I can't prove that you are a bootlicker, then I would become your sex slave for say a month. You could do anything you wanted to me, including sticking it in the old back door or having me suck your cock until you ejaculate in my mouth. Of course, I would swallow everything that spurts out of your tip. You could even take that taws to my ass as many times as you wanted. How does that sound to you?"

It sounded way too good to be true, but he couldn't say that to his wife. But he didn't know how to answer her because he couldn't say 'and if you can prove it' because that would sound like he thought there was a chance she could. He had to keep his story intact that there was no way he had ever licked her boots.

"I am surprised you aren't jumping at this chance, Ray. But just so you understand the entire picture. Let's just assume I can prove that you are, in fact, a bootlicker, then I would expect that you would become my slave at the same time. Of course, I wouldn't want you as a sex slave. It would be disgusting to me to think about a bootlicker making love to me. What I would want would be first to have you fitted with a chastity device so that you couldn't continue to play with yourself. I would also expect that you would do all of the household chores, including cleaning the toilets, showers, and sinks, vacuuming all the rugs, and cleaning out the refrigerator and oven. The tasks are too numerous to mention, but let's just say you would be busy for more hours than you usually have after work. You might even lose a little sleep. What do you say? If you are so sure of yourself, then what do you have to lose? Unless, of course, you are not so sure. Do we have a bet or not?"

Ray figured he had no way out. He had to agree, or it would leave doubt in Rita's mind. "Okay, you have a bet. How do we settle this?"

"Follow me." Rita turned and headed out of the kitchen and towards the stairs.

Not knowing what else to do, Ray did as she suggested and followed her. She entered the bedroom, and to his dismay there on the bed lay her black boots that he had masturbated on just a few hours previously. He knew that he should just ignore them, but now he could not take his eyes off of those boots. He had a tremendous urge to walk over pick them up and start to inspect them. He was now sure that in his haste, he had left some trace of evidence on them.

Rita did not say anything for a short while. She just kept looking back and forth, first to the boots and then to her husband's face. To her delight, she could hear his breathing increase slightly, and she could see small droplets of sweat forming on his forehead. "Is something wrong, dear? You seem to be having some trouble looking away from my boots. Do you know the boots that I asked you about when I came home? The boots that you supposedly went into the closet to look for but came back with my ankle boots instead?"

Rita then put a hand on Ray's back and gave him a nudge toward the bed. "Go ahead, Ray, pick them up and look them over carefully. You are probably wondering if you got all of your cum off of the shafts. Oh, and if you pick them up, you may find my panties that you used to wrap around your cock while you were licking my boots."

Ray knew that he was caught. He just did not understand how she had sprung the trap closed on him so quickly. But he had to try one more time to lie his way out of this. "All that is pure conjecture. Having a pair of boots and a pair of panties on the bed doesn't prove anything."

"Pick them up, Ray. Look at them carefully. Tell me what you see."

Ray did not want to do it, but he found himself obeying nonetheless. He walked over to the bed and picked up first one boot and then the other. He turned them every which way in his hand and looked closely. He could not see any signs of dried cum, but what he did see was that one side of the shaft of each boot was cleaner than the other. In his haste to get rid of the evidence, he had neglected to run the damp towel over the entire surface of the boots. He laid the boots down, carefully ignoring the soiled panties lying under them. Turning to his wife, he spoke.

"I don't see anything strange about your boots. I guess you lost the bet. Take off your robe so I can get started training my new sex slave."

Unbelievingly, Rita did as he asked. She took the belt tie and undid the knot. Slowly, seductively she allowed the robe to fall open, revealing that she was naked underneath. She slid her arms out of the robe and allowed it to fall to the carpet at her bare feet. She reached up and took one breast in each hand and squeezed it. She allowed her thumb to brush lightly over each nipple and felt it hardening with the ministrations. She allowed her tongue to sneak out of her mouth wet her lips and gave Ray a seductive smile.

He started toward her, and for the first time since this whole nightmare began, he felt his cock start to swell in anticipation of what he was going to do to her. As he imagined her bound and helpless and her ass impaled on his cock, he let out a little moan of anticipation. He was reaching for her when she put out a hand and placed it against his chest.

"Not quite so fast, counselor. I haven't rested my case yet. I still have a piece of evidence to present to the jury. Your honor, I introduce into evidence the plaintiff's exhibit 3." And then she pulled her laptop out from under the mattress. She opened the lid and used her finger to stir the built-in mouse. When the screen came to life, she tapped on one of the icons on her desktop, and a video began to play. Ray wanted to run and hide, but instead, he grabbed the computer. Whether he thought that he could simply erase the evidence wasn't clear to him at the time, but it didn't matter as his wife quickly slapped his face.

"Don't even think about erasing that video. Of course, I have already sent it to the cloud for safekeeping. And if you don't do everything that I tell you, from now on, I will be sending it to Facebook and as an email attachment to everyone you know. Do I make myself clear, pervert?"

That was the first time in this entire conversation that Rita had raised her voice, and it had the desired effect. With nothing better to do, Ray sank to his knees and began kissing his wife's feet.

Chapter Fifteen - Charlene Confesses to Jason

The next few days were like heaven for Rita as she took full advantage of her newfound power over Ray. She made sure he had a complete list of chores made up for him before she left the house in the morning and did a complete inspection of the results when she got home. She made sure to find some fault each day, which required a disciplinary session tied to the desk in the basement. And of course, he enjoyed having that mat to lie on as the taws worked on his ass cheeks.

Satisfied that she had put one half of the equation straight, she called her sister and insisted that she take the final step. Charlene balked a little at the suggestion that she talk with her husband, but after a while, she relented and agreed.

As Jason walked into his house, having returned from work, he was greeted by a very contrite wife as he walked in the door. She took his hand and led him into the living room and asked him to sit down. "I have something that I need to discuss with you. And then she handed him a glass half full of straight whiskey. "You will probably need this before I am through." She said.

She began by telling him about discovering her masochistic tendencies when she was a child. She could see the disbelief on his face as she enumerated all of the times that she had found someone to bruise and batter her body. She even told him about a couple of trips to the hospital that her parents had believed were the results of accidents.

When she finally got around to what had led up to her first encounter with her brother-in-law, she could see Jason begin clenching his hands as if he were getting ready for a fistfight. He did smile a little when she told him about catching Ray with his wife's boots in his mouth. But he was not smiling when she gave a graphic blow-by-blow account of the things that Ray had done to her over the years.

"I am going to kill that son of a bitch!" He railed.

Charlene put her arms around her husband's shoulders and tried to calm him. "Please just let this be between the two of us. Ray is being handled by my sister, and believe me when she gets through with him, he will wish you had killed him. But please understand if it had not been Ray; it would have been someone else. I cannot live without some type of pain being administered to me."

Jason held his head in his hands because he did not know what he could do. This woman who he loved more than life itself loved being hurt more than she loved him. And he was positive that he could not be the one to satisfy this terrible wrong desire that she had.

"I thought that you loved me, Charlene." He pleaded.

"I do, as God is my witness. I love you with every fiber of my being. But you don't understand this craving I have for pain. It is like a demon is inside of me, twisting and turning and trying to break through my skin to come out. The harder I try to suppress it, the harder it tries to break free. I have even tried to satisfy him by hurting myself, but it is never enough. How can I make you understand?"

"I don't know that you can. Do you want me to hurt you while I am making love to you? Is that it?"

"I don't want you to make love to me. I want you to savage me as a caveman would to his woman. I want to be tied down and whipped as you drive your cock into my cunt. Or better still drive your cock into my ass until it makes me scream."

"You need help, Charlene. But I am afraid that I am not the one to help you. I think we should call a therapist that specializes in these types of addictions."

"Yes, that is what Rita said as well. I would try it if you went with me. Rita recommended that I call someone she has heard about. She deals with sexual addictions of all kinds and has had some excellent results. I will give her a call if you agree to go with me."

Chapter Sixteen - The Evil Therapist Strikes Again

They did not have to wait long once Charlene explained what her problem was to Dr. Mark's receptionist before she had an appointment. She had no idea what to expect as she and Jason walked into the big medical building and finally into Dr. Marks's office.

After filling out some forms and having her identification and insurance cards copied, she was shown to an inside office. Jason was told to wait until Dr. Marks had a few minutes in private with his wife. As Charlene entered a fairly tall, dark-haired woman arose from behind her desk and came out to greet her. The Doctor held her hand a little longer than she thought was necessary, but she was soon put completely at ease.

They shared a little bit of small talk about how Charlene came to be recommended to her, and then the doctor got right down to business.

"I understand that you have a fetish for pain. Is that correct, dear?"

"I don't know if you would call it a fetish as much as it is a compulsion. I have to have it. I crave it, but fetish seems such a strange word to describe my need."

"So tell me when did this craving first manifest itself to you?"

"Oh, my so far back that I can not ever remember a time when I did not have it. At first, I tried to cause the pain myself. I would take a strap that hung in the kitchen, and when no one was around, I would hit myself on the legs and sometimes over my shoulders. But I was never able to truly satisfy. Then one day I met a boy who liked to tease me. He would do mean things to me like pull my hair or push me down. The rougher he got, the better I liked it. So I would do things to make him angry, knowing that he would retaliate by hurting me

I soon discovered if I called him names like wimp or sissy that he would hurt me even more. We were constantly together, and nobody even suspected what the relationship was all about. He soon found out that I liked being hurt, and he discovered that he liked hurting me, so it was kind of a match made in heaven or maybe more like hell.

One time he hit me with his fist in the face and gave me a huge black eye. Then he got scared thinking that I would rat him out to my parents, but I made up some story about falling when they asked about the eye.

He didn't come around for a while after that, and I had to content myself with whatever pain I could cause myself. And then one day he came around again and asked if everything was cool with my parents. I gave him a big hug and then told him that everything was fine, but from now on, if he was going to hit me with his fist, he needed to do it where it didn't show so much. And then he got into the game. We would go out into the woods, and he would make me take off all my clothes, and then he would either hit me in the stomach or high up on my arms or my legs. That graduated to him, starting to use sticks that he would find and beat me with them.

If my parents happened to see the marks on my body, I would simply pass it off as having fallen down a rocky slope when I was hiking or falling off my bike. They were clueless. They believed everything that I told them.

So for most of my life, I managed to find someone to cause me the pain that I so desired. Up until I married Jason, that is. I tried dropping hints to him, but he never caught them. And once I asked him to beat me with his belt, and he told me that was sick."

Dr. Marks broke in with another question at that point. "So this has been going on for most of your life, right? So why are you seeking professional help now?"

Well, everything came to a head last week. You see, I found out about five years ago that my sister's husband was a sadist. So every time that Rita would go out for the evening, he would call me up, and I would go over for a session. Of course, no one else knew about our arrangement. But then, quite by accident, my husband saw the bruises on my back and the abrasions on my front from where Ray had forced me down on a harsh mat and fucked me from behind."

"What caused the bruises on your back if I may ask?"

"Ray used a heavy taws to beat my shoulders and back as he stroked his cock in and out of my cunt. Oh, I am so sorry for using that language to describe it."

"Think nothing of it. I insist that my patients use common everyday terms to describe their sexual problems. Cock, cunt, tits, ass, and fuck are completely acceptable terms. So continue with your story. Why are you here now?"

"Well, both my husband and my sister think that I am sick and need professional help, and frankly, I can see their point of view. Surely it is not normal for a woman to need to be whipped when she is being fucked to get enjoyment out of it."

"I want to make one thing very clear, Charlene. You are not to blame here. Your husband is the one completely at fault. You have a special need, and he refuses to satisfy it. If he won't or can't because of his selfish nature, you have every right to seek satisfaction outside of the marriage bond. Why can't you continue fucking your brother-in-law?"

"Well, for one thing, my sister would kill me. She was quite understanding when I finally confessed to her, but she is making her husband pay big time. She has turned him into her full-time slave and locked his cock into a chastity device. He won't be fucking me or anyone else anytime soon."

"Then, the answer is quite clear. We either need to convince your husband to man up and take his duties more seriously, or we need to find you someone else to help you out. May I ask a very personal question?"

"Of course."

"Does it have to be a man that hurts you while you are having sex?"

"I am not sure I understand your question, Doctor."

"Well, for instance, if a woman was to use a strap-on to fuck you while she was beating you, would that be sufficient?"

"Oh God, I never thought of anything like that. It would certainly be worth a try, and perhaps it wouldn't bother Jason quite so much if I was with another woman instead of a man."

"Fuck what Jason thinks. If he is not man enough for you, maybe we should turn him into a woman." She then pressed the intercom button and directed her receptionist to send Jason in.

Dr. Marks introduced herself and then got straight to the point. "Your wife has told me about a special need she has, and she tells me that you are unwilling to help her with it. Is that true?"

"If you mean has she told me that she needs to be beaten when we make love, I find that to be beyond anything that a normal person would be able to help her with."

"Then she has no other alternative but to go out and find someone else who will satisfy that need. Are you okay with that?"

"No, of course, I am not okay with that. We are married, and she took a vow to keep herself only unto me until death do us part. I forgave her the indiscretion she committed with her brother-in-law, but I am not going to condone her finding another man to have a kinky affair with."

"Then I will recommend that she retain a good divorce attorney and kick your ass to the curb. You cannot have it both ways. You are going to share in her pain and pleasure, or you are going to be looking for another wife. Perhaps you can find one that fits your normal expectations. So is that what you want? Because if it is, I will make a phone call right now so she can file the proper forms."

"What in the hell kind of a therapist, are you?" Jason railed.

"The kind that does not believe in putting up with male bullshit. None of this is your wife's fault. Every ounce of the blame rests firmly on your shoulders."

"I don't understand what it is that you want me to do?"

"I don't give a damn what you do. It is your wife that needs your compassion. I have already told her that I think she should be looking for someone who loves her enough to help her with this need. You notice that I do not call it a problem because it is not. I can give her the names of a dozen sadists that would be glad to use their whips on her back while they stuff her cunt with a cock that I am sure is much bigger than yours. Of course, the other option would be for you to stop at an adult novelty shop and pick up a good flogger to use yourself."

"I wouldn't know where to begin, even if I did decide that was an option."

"Well, why didn't you say so if that is all you need is a little instruction? I am an expert. How about it Charlene, are you up for a little show and tell?"

"What do you have in mind, Doctor?"

"First, tell Jason what it is that you want from him. And tell him in such a way that he will understand."

Charlene turned to her husband, and in the firmest voice, she could muster announced. "Jason, I want you to whip me while we are making love."

"Charlene, is that really what you meant to say? Did you want to use the words making love?"

"No."

"Then what word did you want to say?"

"Fucking," Charlene said in a soft voice.

"Speak up, slut. I don't think Jason heard you."

"I want you to whip me while we are fucking. Jason, did you hear me that time?"

"So, Jason, now you know what your wife wants. Are you willing to give it to her if I show you how?"

"I will try."

"Good, Charlene, take your clothes off and go bend over that padded bench. I know you would probably prefer something less comfortable, but I guarantee you that you will be in a great deal of pain soon. I am going to hurt you. I am going to hurt you very badly. Is that what you want?"

"Yes."

"When you address me, you will call me Mistress. Do you understand slut?"

Charlene was surprised that she did not take offense when the Doctor used such a derogatory word to address her. She felt her pussy beginning to respond, and she relished hearing even more such words.

"Yes, Mistress, and thank you, Mistress, for recognizing that I am indeed a slut."

Charlene was completely naked and bent over the padded bench, and Jason just stood there fully clothed. "Well, aren't you going to take off your clothes as well, Jason? You can't very well fuck your slut wife if your cock is still covered by cloth."

"Why do you keep referring to Charlene with such ugly names? She is not a slut, and I don't think you are helping her by taking away what little self-respect she has left."

"Charlene knows that she is a slut, and she craves being called a slut. Give her a dollar before you fuck her, and then we can call her a whore. Now get your clothes off, or should I get my strapon?"

Reluctantly Jason began unbuttoning his shirt. Next, he undid the button on his trousers and pulled the zipper down. Finally, he stepped out of his shoes so that he could get his pants off his legs.

"The undershorts as well." The Doctor instructed.

Carrying a heavy flogger, she directed Jason to stand right behind his wife. "Guide the tip of your cock into her cunt and then thrust forward with everything you've got."

Tired of arguing, Jason followed instructions. He didn't even check to see if Charlene was wet. He just drove straight to the hilt. As his hips hit her ass cheeks, Dr. Marks swung the flogger as hard as she could against Charlene's shoulders. The woman let out a scream causing Jason to pull out and step back.

"Get that cock back inside her. She didn't tell you to stop."

"But you hurt her. She can't possibly want anymore."

"Tell him, bitch. Tell him what you want."

"Oh, God, please hurt me. That was so wonderful. Jason, please fuck me while my Mistress whips me."

"You will be the one who decides when the whipping stops Jason." Dr. Marks told him. "When I see cum running down her legs, then I will stop whipping her."

And again and again, the whip rose and fell. Charlene did not scream after the second stroke, and by the tenth, she was moaning but in obvious pleasure. And Jason had got himself into the mood as well. He couldn't believe how good it felt fucking a helpless woman while she was being severely whipped. When he had finally expelled the last drop of cum from his balls, he stepped back just enough so that his spunk could run out of his wife's body. Only then did the whip stop rising and falling. His wife's back was crisscrossed with vicious red welts.

Jason started to turn away but then decided perhaps he was still due something for his aggravation. He grabbed his wife by the hair and pulled her to her feet. When she was standing, he forcefully turned her until she was facing him. Putting one hand on each of her shoulders, he forced her to her knees. "Suck my cock, cunt. And make sure that you swallow every drop of my seed that I ejaculate into your mouth."

Charlene was the most willing cocksucker that Dr. Marks had ever witnessed.

"I think you two are going to be all right. Just make sure you stop and buy that whip on the way home. And while you are in there, get a few pairs of alligator grip nipple clamps. Take Charlene in with you, and I bet she will see a few other toys to take home as well."

Jason turned to Dr. Marks. "Thank you so much for this gift you have given us."

"Oh, it wasn't a gift. Wait till you see my bill. You will be the one in pain then."

She showed Jason out of her office, but she held her hand up in a stop sign position to let Charlene know that she wanted to talk with her in private. When the door had closed behind Charlene's husband, Dr. Marks turned to Charlene.

"Was that all that you had hoped for, slave?" She asked.

"Oh, God, was it? Even Ray couldn't have caused me that much pain. Thank you so much, Mistress."

"Here is the proper way to thank me." And she pulled Charlene into her arms for a passionate kiss. Charlene had never kissed a woman before, and she quickly realized how much she had been missing. Dr. Mark's lips were softer than a man's, her tongue tasted better than any man's she had ever sucked, and her saliva was like the nectar of the gods. She moaned as Dr. Mark's hands started to massage her raw shoulders, and she moaned, more when the Doctor's hands started roughly squeezing her breasts. She was again wet between her legs, and all she could think about was having that whip used again this time on her front.

Dr. Marks pulled back away from her much too quickly for Charlene's liking. "Now slave, you understand that you will never be completely satisfied with your clumsy husband. When the demon inside you becomes more than you can bear, give me a call. There are still wonders for you to explore, starting with how good my cunt will taste."

Charlene could not get that vision out of her mind as the Doctor opened the door and gestured for her to leave.

Chapter Seventeen - Rita Pays The Doctor a Visit

Rita decided to check in on her sister the following day after Charlene's doctor's appointment. It had taken quite a lot of persuading from both Rita and Jason to get Charlene to seek professional help, and Rita was quite curious about how everything worked out.

She made sure that Ray had a full day's housework to do, and then she got in her car and paid a visit to her sister. Rita noticed that there was only one car in the drive when she pulled up and so she figured that Jason must be at work.

Rita pressed the doorbell and waited for her sister to let her in. She was fairly sure that Charlene was home because she could hear music playing inside, and her sister was very frugal when it came to the use of electricity. She would never leave the stereo on if she were not home.

After waiting for what she considered a reasonable length of time, she took the spare key from under the mat and let herself in. She followed the sound of the music to a small room that her sister used as an office. The door was closed, and so she knocked out of respect for her sister's privacy just in case she was doing something of an intimate nature. She thought she heard some kind of sound, perhaps a moan coming from the other side of the door, and so she knocked again louder this time.

When she still did not get a response, she tentatively tried the knob. Finding the door unlocked, she opened it slowly and peered around and into the room. The scene before her completely shocked her, and she rushed into the room. Her sister's hands were tied above her head in such a way that Charlene's toes barely touched the floor. A pink rubber ball gag was fastened behind her teeth with a leather strip that went around behind her head. And then she noticed something that completely shocked her. Two cruel-looking nipple clamps were attached to the ends of Charlene's breasts, and a chain dangled between them. Attached to the chain was a heavyweight, which looked like it was made of lead.

After the initial shock, Rita started towards her sister intending to first release her from the cruel bondage position she was in, but Charlene started to shake her head violently from side to side. Rita took that to mean that she was not to untie her, so she removed the ball gag before she did anything else. As she reached behind her sister to undo the gag, she noticed that her entire back was a mass of crisscrossed welts, and she knew that Charlene had found a replacement for Ray.

As soon as the ball gag was removed from her mouth, Charlene began to speak. It took a second or two to get her tongue to move in the right way, but Rita got the message soon enough.

"Don't you dare let me down. My legs are just beginning to cramp up nicely. And those clamps on my nipples are beginning to burn."

"Those all sound like excellent reasons to let you down, little sister. But I will give you a chance to explain before I do. But if what you say does not make sense, then down you will come. And where in the hell is Jason anyway? Don't you realize how dangerous this is? What if the house caught on fire? You would be helpless. And I have heard that being suspended like you are can cause you to stop breathing."

"Jesus, you are such a worrywart! Jason and I went for a counseling session yesterday as you asked us to do and surprise, surprise the Doctor did not try to talk me out of my obsession with pain. Instead, she told Jason to get on board and help me with my need, or she would find another man who was willing to do so."

"Well, from the looks of your back, Jason took her advice. My God, Charlene, how can you stand that much pain?"

"It wasn't Jason that used the whip on me although he did fuck me while Doctor Marks swung the whip. God, that woman is an expert with the lash."

"I can't believe what I am hearing. Are you saying that Dr. Marks not only talked Jason into hurting you, but she did the damage that I see here?"

"Not all of it but most. You see, she told Jason to stop at a novelty store and buy a whip on the way home. And of course, he had to try it out. And don't you just love these wonderful nipple clamps?"

"Charlene, I am afraid you have a much bigger problem than I realized. I cannot in good conscience leave you hanging there with no one to watch over you."

"Please, I am begging you to leave me here at least for another hour. You can go to the kitchen and have some coffee while you are waiting. But please, I am begging you I need this."

Although Rita figured that she must be as loony as her sister, she agreed but with a caveat. "I am going to call this Doctor of yours. If she agrees to see me before the hour is up, I will have to release you and go. The longer I am left hanging by her receptionist, the longer I will leave you hanging."

Rita poured herself a cup of coffee and sat down at the kitchen table to think. She knew that Charlene always kept important phone numbers on the refrigerator, and sure enough, she found a card under a small magnet with Dr. Mark's phone number on it.

Rita was sure that Dr. Marks would never talk with her about her sister and so she figured she would have to use a little subterfuge to accomplish what she had in mind. She called the office, and when the receptionist asked her what she wanted, she explained that she was writing a book about sexual addictions, and since Dr. Marks was one of the leading psychologists in that field, she would like to set up a time for an interview.

The receptionist said that she would relay the message and then took down Rita's cell number. As Rita hung up the phone, she heard another car pull into the drive. Presently she heard the front door open, and Jason appeared in the kitchen doorway. He nodded at Rita and then poured himself a cup of coffee and sat down across from her.

"I suppose you have already discovered my wife's new pastime. Believe me; we are just following Doctor's orders."

"Yes, so Charlene tells me. What a crock of shit. That therapist must be a quack. She was supposed to convince Charlene to give up her addiction, not get you to beat the shit out of her, and then leave her hanging while you wander around God knows where."

"Look, I know you are concerned for your sister, but you have no call coming over here and getting on my ass because I am trying to do what was recommended."

"What happened to the outrage you had when it was Ray swinging the whip? Now you are doing the same thing that he did and enjoying it."

"Maybe I am enjoying it. Have you ever tried it?"

"Fuck you, Jason. You better make sure that nothing happens to Charlene that time cannot repair."

Still totally pissed, Rita walked out the door and got into her car. She wanted to do a little shopping at the adult novelty store herself as the chastity tube that Ray had picked up was not as secure as she would like it to be. But just as she was pulling into the parking lot, her phone began to ring.

Hitting the accept key, she answered. "Rita Talmadge, how may I help you?"

"Rita the writer I presume," A female voice spoke in her ear.

"Yes, and to whom do I have the pleasure of talking to?"

"Time will tell if it is going to be a pleasure. For now, you are talking with Dr. Loretta Marks. I understand that you want to interview me?"

Rita was shocked that the Doctor had called her back so quickly. In fact, she was astounded that the Doctor had returned her call at all.

"Yes, I would very much like to ask you a few questions for a book I am presently writing. If you can spare me a few minutes, that is?"

"Are you familiar with the Grand Hotel downtown?" Dr. Marks asked.

Strangely enough, that was where the meeting for The Hot Wives Club had taken place, so Rita knew it well. "Yes, I am very familiar with that hotel." She answered.

"Meet me in the hotel bar at say eight this evening. There is a meeting there that I attend now and again. It starts at nine so that would give us an hour. Will that be enough time?"

I am reasonably sure that it is sufficient. If all goes well, perhaps we can schedule a second interview for later."

"Eight, it is then." And the line went dead.

Rita checked her watch and found that it was already late in the afternoon. Since she had not planned on meeting anyone that evening, she had not dressed to thrill, so she figured she should forgo the trip into the novelty store. She decided to test to see how well-trained her husband was becoming, so she called him and told him she would be home shortly and that she wanted him to prepare a hot bubble bath for her. Then as an afterthought, she told him to lay out some of her most sexy clothes just to see what he would come up with. She did not tell him what the occasion was.

She was pleased when she saw how well Ray had done. Not only had he drawn the bath as directed, but he had even added some perfumed oil to the bubbly water. He offered to help her undress, which she readily accepted, and was pleased that he had a look of lust on his face with each item she removed from her body. She hoped that he was undergoing extreme torture with his cock locked up and not being able to remove the tension.

He helped her into the tub, and she commanded him to wash her back for her, and then while he was kneeling by the side of the tub made a big show of washing her breasts and then her pussy. She heard him groan slightly, and she smiled at him and patted his cheek with a sudsy hand. "Are you enjoying your chastity, slave?" She asked although she already knew the answer.

She finally released him to leave the room. She had thought about keeping him there on his knees until she had finished bathing and then making him towel her dry, but there were other chores she had assigned him.

She luxuriated in the hot perfumed water for a little longer than she had intended. She used the time to calm her mind from her confrontation with her brother-in-law and also to prepare her thoughts for how she would approach Dr. Marks later in the evening.

Exiting the bathroom with a large towel wrapped around her, she was amazed to see what Ray had laid out for her to wear for her evening out. She had told him sexy, but she had not expected the garters and real nylons or the crotch-less panties that went with them. He must have hunted through her wardrobe because he had found an old leather mini-skirt, which she had not worn in some time. As she donned the sexy undergarments, she began to feel a little aroused, although she had no intention of anyone seeing her in them. The satin blouse Ray had chosen for her was not see-through, but it was sheer enough so that the outline of the red bra would show through a little.

"Dear Lord, I look hot!" She exclaimed as she looked into the full-length mirror. "Now, what should I wear on my feet?"

But Ray had decided that as well. He came into the room, carrying her favorite black knee-high boots. It was probably no coincidence that they were the same ones that had started Ray on his way to becoming her slave. She smiled as she noticed that they were so highly polished that she could almost see her reflection in them.

"May I help you put on your boots, Mistress?"

"Yes, you may. And I want to compliment you on the wonderful job you have done cleaning and polishing them. I hope you enjoyed doing it as much as I will enjoy wearing them this evening."

He was already on his knees, sliding one of the boots onto her foot. "I did enjoy it very much, and may I say how much I love my new position as your servant, Mistress?"

"I am glad because I am thinking of extending your month of servitude indefinitely. Would you like that slave?"

He hesitated to answer, and she looked down into his eyes. She could not quite read whether he was searching for the right words, or he wanted to avoid the question. Rita knew that it would not be fair for her to unilaterally change the deal she had struck with him, so she patted his cheek and said. "We will talk about it later. No decision needs to be made tonight."

As she drove towards the hotel, Rita thought back on her last words to Ray before she had left the house. It surprised her a little bit to realize that she had not forced an issue that she probably could have won. She enjoyed the servitude that her husband gave her, and she wanted it to continue past the month's deadline that she had set for him. But she also realized that she was no longer angry with him for his betrayal with her sister. She thought he was probably right that few if any men could resist when a beautiful woman wanted them to fuck them. And not too many could resist dishing out a little pain while they did it.

She was still musing on those thoughts when she pulled into the hotel parking lot. She checked her watch and discovered that she was about 15 minutes early for her meeting with Dr. Marks. She figured that she would use the time to have a stiff drink before the other woman arrived. It would quell the nerves floating throughout her body.

She chose a stool at the bar, knowing that she would get quicker service there. As she sat down, the leather skirt she was wearing rode up her thighs, exposing her stocking tops, and she wished that she had chosen a looser fitting if not a longer skirt. She looked around and found that every male in the place was looking her way. Most of them had their eyes aimed directly at her exposed flesh, and so it took them a little while to realize that they had been caught staring. One man, however, caught her eye and held it. He was by far the best-looking piece of male meat she had ever seen before. His eyes were dark and shiny, and he seemed to be able to look deep into her soul. He had a smile on his face that made her feel weak in the knees and lips that were made for kissing. His dark hair was longer than most men wore theirs, but it was not feminine in any way. An image crossed her mind of her hands running through that thick hair as those lips descended upon hers. She saw him get to his feet and head her way, and she was afraid that she would not be able to refuse this man anything he wanted. And just then her savior arrived

She heard her name, and it snapped her out of her daydream of illicit sex. She snapped her head to the side, breaking eye contact with the male God who was heading her way. She forced herself to look fully upon the woman who stood beside her stool. "You must be Rita, I presume?" The woman asked, but as if she already knew the answer.

"And you must be Doctor Marks?" She replied.

"Please call me Loretta. All my friends do, and I imagine you will be added to that list shortly. Why don't you bring your drink over to the corner booth where we can talk in relative privacy? Oh, and you might want to give your number to the male distraction you were devouring with your eyes as I walked up."

Loretta motioned for the man to step forward, and when he did, she addressed him. "Go ahead and give her your number but be quick about it. That bulge in your pants will have to wait until later tonight."

The man gave her a big smile, which, for some reason, caused a small bout of jealousy to rise into Rita's throat. She quickly jotted her number down on a napkin and passed it to the man. She had never done anything like that before, and she felt her cheeks begin to redden in embarrassment. The man took the napkin from her hand and then brought that same hand to his lips and planted a gentle kiss on the back. "My name is Damion, and may I ask what yours might be?"

"Rita." She simply replied.

"Ah, such a wonderful name. It means Pearl in some languages, and it is quite fitting for such a beautiful gem like you. May I be so bold as to ask if it is okay for me to give you a call later this evening?"

Rita knew that she was playing with fire, but the heat between her legs would not allow her to say no. Please do, although it may be quite late before I finish with a prior engagement.

"I would wait all night and many more nights for the privilege of holding your hand."

Rita blushed and excused herself, knowing that at that moment, it was not her hand she needed to be held.

She knew that her face was aglow with passion as she sat down across from Loretta Marks. The older woman looked deeply into her eyes. "This must be your first time playing this game. You are so flushed that one would think you were in the throes of an orgasm just from having that man touch your hand."

Rita could not believe how close her new acquaintance was to the truth. "You are a very observant woman, Loretta. But I didn't come here to talk about my sexual proclivities."

"No, you wanted to talk about your sister's addiction to pain, I believe."

Rita was stunned. She had no idea how this woman had deciphered this. "I am not sure what you are referring to." She tried to lie.

"You must think that I just fell off the turnip truck yesterday, my dear. Did you not realize that Charlene would have to fill out a complete family history when she came in for treatment? And of course, you look almost identical to her though perhaps a little older and a little sexier. And incidentally, I love that skirt you are wearing. And red is such a wonderful color for a garter belt."

Once again, Rita's face turned red, and she saw Loretta chuckle just a little bit. "You are new to this game. It is a little surprising since you write books about sex. I would have thought that you would have had a lot of experience with the subject."

Rita gave a little laugh. "Not so much, it seems. That is why I need to do so much research."

"Okay, let's get all the recriminations out of the way. Perhaps we will have some time to talk about what you want to do with that gorgeous piece of meat you just met."

"Okay, you are right. I guess I did come here to confront you about how you treated or did not treat Charlene. I thought for sure you would at least try to show her how dangerous her desire for pain could be, but instead, you suggest that her husband begin beating her. I found her dangling from a hook they had put in the ceiling this morning. She was stretched so tight that only her toes were touching the ground, and her leg and foot muscles were already starting to spasm. And her back was a mass of welts that she told me you put there. What kind of therapist are you?"

"The kind that realizes that sometimes a person is better off accepting their addictions than trying to cure them. Can Charlene be cured? I doubt it. She has been living with this addiction for far too many years. Perhaps with years of therapy and perhaps even being institutionalized, we might be able to lessen her urges, but at some point, something will bring that longing back to the surface, and she will once again begin looking for relief from the demon inside her. I am a little concerned with the condition you say you found her in this morning. That is indeed dangerous to be left hanging like that without supervision. I need to have another talk with her and Jason to make sure he at least understands what is and is not acceptable. And of course, if you were a loving sister, you might volunteer to watch over her when she needs strict bondage."

"Now wait just a minute. Surely you are not suggesting that I should become involved in hurting my sister?"

"Why not, you have done it in the past."

Rita thought back to their childhood and realized that the Doctor was right at least to some degree. But back then, she thought they were just roughhousing or sometimes fighting. She did not realize that her sister was pushing her buttons to get the pain she desired.

"Suppose that I accept the fact that Charlene has to have this kind of treatment. Surely there are other ways of causing her pain that are not so dangerous. How about those nipple clamps she was wearing this morning? Those looked extremely painful. How long could she wear those without danger?"

"As with any constrictive device shutting off the blood supply can cause lasting damage. Normally they should not be left on for more than 15 minutes. So you see, once again, supervision is necessary. One thing you could try is to put some uncooked rice in the bottoms of her high-heeled boots and make her walk on it all day. That would probably be enough pain to satisfy her between her whippings. Another thing you could try would be to put a little menthol directly inside her labia while her hands were tied behind her back. There are even more cruel types of creams that can be used, although I will not endorse any particular brand. And of course, they all cause some drying of the tissue so they shouldn't be left on indefinitely.

Itching powder is another idea. Although it is not painful unless you allow the recipient to scratch, it is distracting and can take the place of pain. Once again, the victim needs to be bound and supervised, however. Something that you might also want to try is to have her lay on a bed of stinging nettles. They are quite painful, but you do need to have some anti-histamine on hand to bring down the welts once you have finished. I suggest you join some of the sadomasochistic forums on the Internet. There are thousands of ideas, most of which I have not tried."

Rita sat back in her chair and took a long pull off of the drink she had before her. She was more confused now than she was before this meeting began. She had been so sure that she could convince the Doctor of the error of her ways, but now she found herself thinking of ways to safely cause her sister pain.

"If there is nothing more that you want to ask about Charlene, I would be interested in what you are doing with Raymond. Is it Raymond or Ray?"

"What makes you think I am doing anything with my husband?"

"You seem to be a master at answering a question with a question. Charlene told me that you had discovered that she had been having a sadomasochistic affair with her brother-in-law, and I assumed that might have upset you slightly."

"It seems my sister was very open about airing all our dirty laundry in public. Yes, I was pissed when she told me about what she had been doing with my husband. And at the time, I assessed the vast majority of the blame on his shoulders, but I see now that it was Charlene who was completely to blame."

"Now just a minute!" The doctor interrupted. "While Charlene may well have initiated the first act, she did not put a gun to your husband's head and force him to stick his cock into her cunt while he beat her. Charlene had a sexual compulsion that made it very difficult for her to refuse that type of treatment, but what is Ray's excuse? And you don't strike me as the type of woman that would let him get away with betraying you the way he did. I am surprised that you are not wearing his balls around your neck for a necklace."

Rita broke out laughing. All the tension she had felt was gone from her being. The mental picture of Ray's testicles dangling from her neck from a chain caused her amusement.

"No, but in all honesty, I have locked up his cock so he will not be able to repeat his actions until I release him."

"Dear God, woman, why in hell would you ever release him? His cock should never again see the light of day unless it is to be cleaned and only then under strict supervision."

"Yes, well, I made a deal with him, and I never go back on my word. Well, hardly ever at least. I sentenced him to a month's worth of chastity, and unless I can find some way of getting him to agree to a longer term, I will have to release him when the month is over."

"Send him in to see me. I will turn him into a full-time slave for you."

"And you could make all those things happen?"

"Of course for a price. The vast majority of my patients are women who have decided that they would rather have the male in their life as a servant rather than a lover."

"I would think that there might be some ethical problems with that. Hasn't anyone ever reported you for abuse of your position?"

"Is that what this conversation is all about? Are you a whistleblower who wants a shot at my license, Rita?"

"No, of course not. Although I find some of the things you say to be completely bazaar and I am still not 100% sure that you are not full of shit with your diagnosis of my sister, I have no animosity towards you. I would love to spend some time with you so that I could pick your brain some more. But, in this day and age, when everybody sues everybody over everything, I would think you would have run into some serious legal issues."

"You might be right except for three things. First, I am exceptionally good at what I do. Second, in all my years of practice, not one woman who has come to me for help with her marital problems has ever left with a bad taste in her mouth. The vast majority of them leave with huge smiles on their faces?"

"Well, that may be completely true, but what about the men? Surely some, if not all of them are unhappy with the results."

"You did not let me finish. I said there were three things, not two. The third thing is that men are irrelevant."

"How can you say such a thing? Do you think that men are somehow some lower form of life that they do not matter?"

"That is exactly what I think. I believe that there is nothing wrong with the male species as long as a strong, powerful woman controls them. But that is not the reason I said they are irrelevant. They are irrelevant because men have too much pride to admit that they are such pussies that a woman can abuse them. It is extremely rare when a male brings charges of abuse against a woman. And the few that do are usually dismissed. Now you said you might like to spend time with me to pick my brain. Well, you have an excellent opportunity right here tonight. Have you ever heard of a group called The Hot Wives Club?"

"As a matter of fact, I have. I am interviewing a few of their members for my new book dealing with cuckolding."

"Well, I am going to be speaking to them in a few minutes, and I would be happy to extend you an invitation to listen in."

"I would like that very much. I guess tall, dark, and handsome will have to wait."

"Normally, I would say bring him along, but in this group, males are the enemy, and enemies are not allowed at group functions unless it is for show and tell."

"Show and tell, what is that?"

"Oh, once every couple of months, the ladies all bring their slaves with them and show off how well they have them trained. For some, it is just to show off their maid's uniforms. There is even an annual contest for the best-dressed slave. For others, it is to show off how well their male can withstand pain. They have whipping contests where most of the women take turns wielding a whip to see which male can last the longest. It is a great deal of fun. But, I see that it is almost time for the meeting to begin. Come on in and have a seat."

Chapter Eighteen - The Evil Therapist Speaks To The Group

As Dr. Marks was introduced to the group, she got a rousing round of applause. Rita thought that perhaps Loretta was right and that the vast amount of women did find her ways to be appealing. Rita watched with interest as Dr. Marks strode confidently to the podium and began her lecture.

"It pleases me greatly to see so many powerful women gathered here this evening. Most of you are here because you have embraced the truth that you belong to a superior species that we will call women. And the vast majority of you have also embraced the fact that as a superior species, you deserve to be worshipped, adored, and most importantly obeyed by the lesser beings we shall refer to as males. Now some want to call these lesser beings men, but we will not. That species died out many generations ago. They used to rule the world with an iron hand, and they kept the women under their thumbs, not allowing them to vote or to interact in any meaningful way, except to lie on their backs and spread their legs.

Now do not take my meaning wrong. There is absolutely nothing wrong with lying on your back and spreading your legs, as long as it is your idea. And as long as you insist that you receive more pleasure than any male that might be with you. Of course, I would also suggest that you would receive far more pleasure if when you spread your legs, it be for another woman, but we will leave that remark for another lecture."

Rita joined right in with the raucous laughter that resonated throughout the room. Loretta took a drink of water from the glass kept under the podium while she waited for the noise to die down in the room.

"Now the real reason we are here tonight is to encourage those of you that are in attendance to recruit new members to the group. We need you to spread the word among those women, you know. That is the only way that they can have a meaningful existence is if they embrace their feminine power and take control not only of their own lives but the lives of their male companions as well.

For far too long, we have allowed our petty differences to hold us back from our proper positions in this world. Many years ago, our species became the more populous species, and we should have been able to elect women to every position of power, at least within this country. But for the most part, we have had difficulty agreeing on this issue. There are still far too many women out there who will not support other women because they somehow are sticking to what they have been taught in the past by the male-dominated society.

It is my firm belief that sometime in the not-too-distant future women will rule this country. I look forward fondly to the day when males will no longer have any rights of their own in the same way they denied women those rights in the past. I look forward to the day when men will not have the right to vote or to hold office in any capacity in this country, including serving on the boards of companies or corporations. I look forward to a time when males will not be allowed to own property or money. That all such property will be under the firm control of the superior female species."

As she took another sip of water, Rita waited for the members of the audience to begin filing out in protest over the outlandish things they were hearing. But to her surprise and perhaps even dismay, she heard people begin to clap. And soon, the entire audience was on their feet chanting here, here in the form of agreement. It seemed like the ovation would go on forever, but it finally died down. As each of the women returned to their seats, the Doctor again began to speak.

"But the only way we will ever get to that point is if women like you help us to recruit new members to the cause. And it cannot be done simply within the confines of a political movement. Only when you have shown every woman that you know the value of taking control of each male within her circles will she have a chance to succeed. Women need to understand that they do not need a male to be validated, and especially they need to understand that no one male will ever be able to satisfy them sexually. By a show of hands, could I ask how many of you women here tonight have taken complete control of your marriages by turning your husbands into cuckolds?"

She waited for a response, and Rita was again shocked to see almost every hand in the room go up.

"It is truly gratifying to see so many of you have taken this important first step in completely dominating the lesser species. Make no mistake about it until a male learns that his wife, fiancée, or girlfriend is in complete control over her sexuality; he will believe he is in control. From the first time that he sees that you are willing to go to someone else for your pleasure, he will begin to understand his position as a lesser being. How many of you have taken the added step of locking your husband's sexual organ up in a chastity device?"

Again very few hands were not raised. Loretta looked directly at Rita, forcing her to think about her circumstances, and then she shyly raised her hand as well.

"I hope that I am not confusing anyone here by the use of the term husband. I use that term to describe any male that is in a committed relationship whether or not they have taken vows in front of a clergyman or an officer of the court. If a male is not in a committed relationship, he cannot be cuckolded.

One last question, how many times per month should your male be allowed out of his chastity device to relieve his sexual tensions? Anyone?"

It quickly became obvious that most were unsure of what the correct answer might be. So finally, Monica raised her hand. "The correct answer to your question is zero. Once a woman takes control of a male's sex organs, they should never be used again for self-gratification. If she desires to use that organ for her pleasure, then hopefully he has been properly trained in self-control."

"Thank you, Monica, that was an excellent answer to my question. However, it is important to remember that every woman is in charge of her relationship, and there are no hard and fast rules other than she should always do what gives her the most pleasure. That ends my lecture for this evening, but before we close, I would like to ask if there are any questions that anyone would like to ask."

Rita looked around the room and presently saw the hand of a young woman that she had seen at the last meeting go up.

"Hi, my name is Laura, and I am engaged to be married in just two weeks. My mother believes that I should be looking to take a lover before I get married. What is your take on that?"

"That is a difficult question to answer without a little more information. However, I will say that if you truly want to have a long and satisfying marriage, you need to set the ground rules as early as possible. Have you talked with him at all about what you expect from him sexually?"

"Well, to be perfectly honest with you, until my mother insisted on my meeting and talking with some of the other ladies here, I thought she was bonkers. So no, I have not talked with him about becoming my cuckold as you put it."

"Bonkers, huh? Yes, we get that reaction a lot. I met a young woman this evening, that is in attendance. Don't worry, Rita, I won't embarrass you by pointing you out. Although, that is a lovely leather mini that you are wearing. I noticed her frowning at some points during the discourse, so I am sure she is still of the opinion that I am Looney Tunes. Sorry, Rita, that was all in fun. But getting back to your question Laura, you need to find out how much he is in love with you. If he does not love you enough to be able to handle seeing you with other men, then he probably is going to be more trouble than he is worth. Unless you are prepared to go through your entire life being sexually frustrated, you have to bring other people into your relationship. One woman can easily keep a male satisfied. They are pretty much relegated to only having one or two orgasms per night, and that is only while they are young. But you, my dear, can have as many orgasms as you desire."

"Okay, then what should I do to find out before I get married? I certainly do not want to go through with the ceremony and then find out he cannot handle it."

"Unfortunately, there is not enough time to figure it all out in just two weeks. It usually takes several years to properly train a male to become a good cuckold. You have to start with little things and work yourself up to the main event. So in your case, my advice is to go ahead and go through with the marriage. Of course, if you own any property or have funds of your own, you would want to protect them with some kind of prenuptial agreement. If, however, he has sufficient funds, you should make sure that the lion's share of them would go to you in case of dissolution of the marriage."

"You said to start with small things. What would be something small that you would recommend?"

"Do you like to dance?"

"Yes, very much."

"Then insist that he take you dancing. Wear something very sexy so that you will attract attention and so you should have plenty of people asking you to dance. Accept all the invitations you get even if it means your male has to sit out some of the dances. Allow your dance partner to hold you real close and maybe even let him rest his hands on your ass. See how your male reacts to this. At first, he will probably be jealous and make a fuss but be firm with him, explaining that you enjoyed the attention, and he should be happy to see you having a good time if he loves you. Always throw out that caveat, 'if he loves you.'"

Laura thanked the Doctor and then sat back down in her seat. Rita looked her way and wondered if this was the best thing to suggest to a young, almost bride. Hell, she even wondered if it was the best thing for Rita.

Chapter Nineteen - Rita Takes A Chance

As the meeting began to break up, Rita waited for an opportunity to speak with Dr. Marks. It took a while because there were so many women who were thanking Loretta for such an enlightening speech and patting her on the back for a job well done. But finally, she got an opportunity and stepped forward and held out her hand.

"I just wanted to let you know that I enjoyed your speech very much although I may still think you are Looney Tunes. That is the correct scientific term for bonkers is it not?"

Dr. Marks took Rita's hand and gave it a firm shake. "Yes, you have the scientific vernacular down pat. I hope I didn't embarrass you too much by mentioning you. After all, I imagine no one had any idea who I was talking about."

"Yes, I noticed there were so many other newcomers wearing a leather mini. But, no Loretta, I do not embarrass easily. Perhaps we can get together again over drinks sometime."

"Sure but next time, perhaps it could be in private, and when we have enough time to get to know one another." And then Loretta did something shocking to Rita. She reached out and cupped her face with one of her hands drew her in, and kissed her on the lips. It was not just a friendly kiss either as she allowed her tongue to tease the younger woman's lips.

Rita was so confused that she did not resist for a moment, and before she could pull away, Loretta released her face and stepped back. "Yes, you will do quite nicely." She said as she turned back to the other women waiting to speak with her.

Rita was still a little bit in a daze as she wobbled out of the room. As she cleared the doorway and moved to the side to stop and steady herself, her phone began to ring. She had forgotten all about Damion and his promise to call her, but when she answered she recognized his voice.

"Hello, beautiful, I was hoping to get a chance to see you again this evening." The voice in her earpiece said.

"Really and just why would you want to do that?" Rita said it with just a hint of a tease.

"Well, I can think of several reasons but why not talk about them in person? I am just to your left at the bar."

Rita felt her heart begin to flutter knowing what she was about to do. For the past five years, the only man she had been in bed with was her husband Ray. But now she had made up her mind that he was not going to be the only cheater in their marriage.

Her mind was crystal clear on her intent as she made her way towards the bar. She could feel a little bit of moisture beginning to form between the lips of her pussy and she didn't mind if he could smell her scent when she reached him. She allowed her eyes to roam once again over his body imagining the muscles that resided just below the clothes that he wore. She was near to him before her eyes finally got up to his face and she could see that both his lips and his eyes were smiling back at her. He had a quizzical look and she wondered what he must be thinking of this woman that was so blatantly checking him out.

"Do you like what you see beautiful?" He asked. His voice sounded just a slight bit huskier than it had on the phone.

"Very much." Was her reply.

He patted the stool beside her and watched carefully as she climbed atop it. She knew that the tight leather skirt she was wearing was sliding up revealing a lot more of her legs than she would normally feel comfortable with. She looked down and noticed that the ends of her red garters were showing. Turning her head slightly towards Damion she could see a bulge in the front of his slacks and she could almost imagine how big the member causing it was becoming.

Without taking his eyes off her legs, Damion pushed a full glass her way. This made Rita just a little nervous because she had no idea when that drink had been ordered or what might have been slipped into it. She was extra cautious anytime that she drank anywhere but in her own home. She had heard of too many cases of Rohypnol or some other date rape drugs being slipped into unsuspecting women's drinks. She slid it back away from her on the bar trying not to be too obvious about it.

Damion looked at her curiously. "I thought that you might like a little something to loosen you up. I asked the bartender what you were drinking earlier. I hope you don't mind?"

"I am plenty loose without more alcohol. So tell me are you staying here at the hotel?"

"I am why do you ask?"

"Well, if we are going to get to know each other I just thought it should be in a room and not in the bar."

"Wow, you don't waste much time, do you? But I have to inquire about the ring on your finger. It appears to be a wedding ring."

"Is that a problem?"

"It might be, I am not sure yet. "I have this thing for not wanting to move in on another man's property."

Rita thought about trying to smooth things over with this man. She wanted to feel his hard cock deep within her cunt tonight but then she remembered what Dr. Marks had said earlier about being in control of her pussy and not some male.

"So, I look like property to you? What if my husband was to rent me out to you for the night or maybe he could lease me to you for a few days?" Rita's voice had risen so that several of the other customers in the bar were taking notice.

"I didn't mean to insult you. It is just that dealing with angry husbands is not my thing."

Rita reached into her clutch and pulled out her phone. She pushed the button for her husband's cell and waited for Ray to answer. "Hello, slave." She began when he picked up her call. "I am in a hotel bar downtown, and the man that I am about to fuck was worried that you might object. I am putting him on the phone so that he will know that you do not care, understood?"

She handed the phone to Damion, and he tentatively said hello as he put it to his ear. He could hear what sounded like sobbing on the other end, but no one spoke through the earpiece. He handed the phone back to Rita and stood up from his stool. "I am sorry I can't do this." He said.

Rita also stood up from her stool. "I am sorry too. I was looking forward to an entire night fucking your brains out."

She had lost her sexual buzz as she walked away, but she knew that she would not be going home that night. She had set Ray up to think that she was being fucked, and she wanted him to spend the entire night agonizing over that thought. She decided to stop at the front desk and get herself a room for the night. She was in a daze and was not looking where she was going, and she bumped solidly into Loretta Marks.

"Oh, I am so sorry." Rita began to apologize. "I guess I wasn't watching where I was going."

"No harm is done. I kind of moved into your way on purpose."

Rita looked at her and cocked an eyebrow seeking some kind of an explanation.

"Oh, I heard the end of your conversation. I suspect that everyone in the room heard the end of your conversation. I am a little surprised at your male acquaintance. Most men are like dogs; they don't care who they fuck. If I had a suspicious mind, I would wonder if he did not have another alternative motive for trying to ply you with alcohol before taking you to his room."

"I was a little suspicious myself when he had a drink all ready for me when I got to the bar. It is a damn shame I was really in the mood to get laid tonight."

"I was hoping that perhaps I could help you with that," Loretta said with a smile.

Chapter Twenty - Rita Tries New Things

"And precisely how did you figure to do that?"

"I have a room here at the hotel with a very large king-size bed and no one to share it with. I thought perhaps we could try it out together."

Rita let out a small gasp. She had not even considered going where the good Doctor was suggesting she go. "Wow, that caught me by surprise. I have never even thought about doing it with another woman. I wouldn't know where or how to begin."

"Let's begin by going up to my room and having a drink from the mini-bar. All the bottles and sealed, I assure you."

"Well, just thinking about what you suggested, I could certainly use a drink. Why not lead the way."

Rita had no idea what to expect as Loretta slid the keycard into the slot and opened the door. She entered the room and looked around and found that this was one of the more deluxe hotel rooms she had ever visited. The first thing that she noticed was that the first room she came to did not have a bed. Instead, it was furnished like you might expect a living room to be. Three plush chairs, a sofa, and a glass and marble coffee table adorned the room.

Rita watched as Loretta walked across the room to the mini-bar and bent over to select a couple of small bottles of alcohol for them to consume. She had noticed that the Doctor was well dressed when they had met earlier in the bar and again when she had walked to the podium to begin her lecture. But now Rita was examining the older woman in a whole different light. She was trying to imagine what she would be like as a sexual partner, and Rita's eyes stayed a little longer than they should on the woman's ass.

"It is hard to picture, isn't it, dear?"

Rita shook her head to clear it, knowing that she had been caught in the act of staring. "I am sorry, what do you mean?"

"You are trying to size me up much as you would a man, but there is no comparison, so you are unsure as to what you should be looking for."

"Am I that easy to read for you?" Rita asked.

"Well, it is pretty easy to see that you are scared half out of your mind and wondering what the hell you are doing up here with this perverted old woman. But then, looking back, I was probably just as scared my first time out."

"Your first time, were you sure that it was what you wanted to do?"

"Yes, I think so. Of course, I always found women to be more attractive than men."

"And therein lies the rub," Rita stated. "I have never even considered a woman as a sexual partner until you mentioned it downstairs. I am amazed that I didn't run a hundred miles an hour away from you."

"Just relax. Let's have a drink, and we can talk. You sit there in one of the chairs, and I will sit way over here opposite from you. Let's just see where this goes, shall we?"

"That sounds good to me," Rita said as she accepted the small bottle of liquor from Loretta. As her companion sat down across from her, she opened the bottle and took a small sip. The raw taste of the strong spirit burned her throat as it went down, but it also created some warmth that made her feel more comfortable as well.

Loretta didn't say anything as she too opened her bottle and took a sip. She did begin swinging her foot gently back and forth, her shoe dangling just off the ends of her toes. The light from the lamp seemed to be dancing on the toe of that shoe, which Rita somehow found to be entrancing. For some reason, Rita found that swinging foot to be fascinating, and she couldn't take her eyes off of it. Somewhere in the distance, she could hear Loretta's voice, but she couldn't seem to quite make out what it was she was saying. Her eyes began to get very heavy, and she felt her head begin to settle down towards her chest. And then she felt nothing at all as she settled into a heavy sleep.

She had no idea how much time had passed while she slept. When she opened her eyes, she noticed that the room was dimly lit with a red light. She also quickly came to realize that she was no longer in the chair but rather lying on her back in a very comfortable bed. She tried to sit up, but she was unable to do so. She felt cold, and she tried to reach for some covers, but her hands would not move. It became obvious to her that her hands were restrained in some fashion over her head towards where the headboard of the bed would be.

She was now fully awake, and she could tell that she was completely naked. She could feel goosebumps forming on her skin, and her nipples were as hard as small pebbles. She wanted to cry out, but something was inside of her mouth, stopping her tongue from forming words. She knew that her legs were spread wide apart, and she tried to pull them closer together only to discover that each ankle was tied firmly to the bottom corners of the bed.

She had no memory of leaving the chair or how she had gotten into her present position, and she began to be frightened. Surely she thought Loretta could not be responsible for this. Perhaps someone had broken into the room, and the doctor was herself in danger.

Her eyes had now adjusted to the dim red light, and she could see off to her left that someone was sitting in a chair watching her. She turned her head to get a better view, and she now saw that the person was, in fact, Loretta.

"I am glad to see that you are now awake so that we can get started. I could see earlier that you were uncomfortable with the idea, so I thought I would help you along. I am going to remove the gag from your mouth. Your first instinct will be to scream, but I am ordering you not to do that. If you understand, nod your head."

Rita felt compelled to follow the woman's instructions, and so she gently nodded her head up and down.

"Good girl," Loretta told her as she slowly walked towards the bed. She bent over and gave Rita a small kiss on her cheek and then one on her forehead before reaching behind her head and releasing the strap holding the small ball gag in her mouth. Loretta gently extracted the gag and then bent down and kissed Rita on the lips this time.

Rita did have the urge to scream, but for some reason, her promise not to was important to her, and she remained silent. Loretta then pushed a button, and the head of the bed began to rise. "I want you to be able to see everything in a more comfortable position than laying flat on your back. When Rita was sitting upright, the woman stepped back and walked to the foot of the bed. She was back far enough so that Rita could see her entire body, including the black high heels she wore on her feet.

"Now, Rita, I am going to begin to undress for you. I want you to concentrate on the fact that I am your lover who is disrobing for the first time for you. Concentrate on which items of clothing you most want to see taken off of my body. Watch my hands and think about how much pleasure those hands might be able to give you if they were not busy with buttons and clasps."

Rita was mesmerized as Loretta reached for the top button of her blouse. The woman's hands looked so sensuous as she slowly and seductively pushed the button from the eyelet. Loretta licked her lips before moving down to button number two, and Rita imagined how good those lips would taste against hers. Again that tongue snaked out of her mouth, and Rita gave out a little groan of frustration at not being able to get up and go to Loretta. Another button opened, and now Rita could see just the faint outline of Loretta's breasts.

She imagined being able to take those globes into her hands, massaging them wishing that she could see more than just the tops. Another button was pushed from its' eyelet, and now Rita could see the black lace bra holding those delectable breasts in place. A little moisture was collecting between her pussy lips, and warmth was spreading throughout her body. She let out a little moan of pleasure as she watched the next button being undone. "Please, I need to touch you." She begged.

"All in good time, little one. For now, just watch and dream of what will be."

Finally, the blouse was fully opened and pulled from the hem of Loretta's skirt. Now Rita was sure that Loretta would undo the clasp of her bra and allow those globes to fall free so that Rita might gaze on them. But to her chagrin, Loretta reached for the button to the top of her skirt. Slowly swaying back and forth, she teased Rita with the thought that she would drop the skirt but then redid the button. Smiling, she reached behind her and then turned so that her back was to Rita. Her fingers played with the clasp of her bra for so long that Rita was moaning in frustration. "For God's sake, you are killing me with all this anticipation. I either need to touch you or you damn sure need to start touching me. My cunt is on fire."

"Are you sure that is what you want me to do? Where do you want me to touch you, or where do you want me to allow you to touch me?

Rita could not believe how badly she wanted to feel another woman's hands on her body. She was positive that Loretta must have hypnotized her, giving her a suggestion to desire lesbian contact. But right then, she did not care how the thoughts got into her mind. She only wanted those desires fulfilled as rapidly as possible.

"Please, I cannot stand this much longer. I need to be touched. I am on fire with desire."

"My you have become quite a poet. But you just can't rush these things. She did, however, unsnap her bra and allow her breasts to drop free from their restraint. With a smile on her face, she began to play with her globes, and the only thing that Rita could play with was her mind. She wanted to scream when Loretta finally released her skirt and allowed it to hit the floor. She stepped out of it, and Rita was hoping that she would now come and untie her, but instead, she began to rub herself through the thin fabric of her panties, driving Rita just a little more insane.

Loretta let a little moan escape her lips as she moved the panties to the side and dipped two fingers into her now steaming cunt. Rita could smell her sex even though she was a good 10 feet away, and she knew that Loretta was almost as excited as she was.

"Dear God, please. If someone must play with your sex, let it be me. Please, I am begging you."

I love to hear you beg. If I were to grant you your wish, what would you do for me in return?"

"Anything, I will do anything, just untie my hands and come over here."

"You will get your turn, but first, I need to discover your erogenous zones." Loretta finally moved to the bed and bent down so that her lips just grazed Rita's. She allowed her tongue to snake out but only for show. She wet her lips and came close to Rita's but did not make contact. Sitting on the edge of the bed, she reached out and gently began to stroke the side of one of Rita's breasts. Her touch was like a feather, but each inch of flesh she touched was set to tingling.

Rita wanted to scream, "the nipples damn you the nipples," but she bit down hard on her lower lip to keep from giving the other woman the pleasure of hearing her beg.

After what seemed like hours and every inch of Rita's tits covered except for her nipples, Loretta moved further down Rita's body. This time it was her inner thighs that were getting the attention. And like before, the touch was feather soft and just beyond any contact with Rita's sex. She was so wet that she was afraid she was going to soil the coverlet as she thrashed her hips up and down and right and left, trying to get some contact with Loretta's fingers.

And when she was at her very peak of arousal and frustration, Loretta's hand disappeared. Loretta pushed the bed control button and allowed the bed to again fully recline. Quickly the Doctor shifted up onto the bed on her knees. Her dripping snatch was positioned directly above Rita's lips.

The only pussy that Rita had ever tasted was a little of her own when she had experimented by sucking some of her juice off of her fingers when she was first learning to masturbate. It was not an unpleasant taste, but it had not been something that she enjoyed enough to continue to do it. And she knew that small taste would be nothing like what she was about to do.

Loretta slowly lowered herself down towards Rita's lips, and her aroma came to Rita's nose. She willingly breathed in the scent and found that the aroma caused her even more excitement. Now not waiting for Loretta to make her move, Rita quickly raised her head and brought her lips against Loretta's pussy. Loretta moved away but only for a short time, and then she lowered herself down fully on Rita's mouth.

Rita immediately allowed her tongue to snake out and began slowly licking along those wet puffy lips. Hearing a groan come from Loretta's mouth rewarded her, and she felt so satisfied. Driving her tongue even deeper inside the older woman, she reveled in the amount of moisture she was bringing into her mouth. She wished that her hands were free so that she could use them to give more pleasure, but since they were not, she pushed her nose forward and made contact with the swollen bud at the top of Loretta's slash. Hearing Loretta moan again, she moved as violently back and forth with her face as her constricted body would allow making sure that each pass her nose brushed that nub.

Rita now had forgotten all about her arousal. Her only concern now was giving pleasure to her partner. Her tongue was now as far inside Loretta as it could get, and her nose was pressed firmly against the woman's clit. Rita could feel Loretta begin to tense up, and then a loud scream arose from the woman's throat as she began to violently thrash against Rita's mouth and nose. Rita did not stop licking the juices running into her mouth until finally, Loretta lifted off of her and, with a sigh, got off the bed.

"God, that was a good ride. You will make one hell of a cunt licker by the time I am through with you. But now I suppose you need a little attention yourself. I never did care too much for reciprocation, but I do have a surprise for you. Come on in; she is all yours."

Rita had no idea who she might have been talking to, but presently Damion was beside the bed. He was naked, and his huge cock stood up straight away from his body. Seeing the confusion on Rita's face, the man remarked. "Sorry for the subterfuge, but Loretta insisted I give her first crack at you. But now it is my turn, and I hope that I do not disappoint."

Rita did not answer, and she could not move, so all she could do was lie there as he got between her legs. He inserted one finger into her cunt and could tell that she was so wet that no preliminaries were needed. Positioning his cock at the entrance to her tunnel, he pushed it in about two inches and then stopped to allow her to become accustomed to his girth. Rita, however, had waited as long as she was going to, and with one upward thrust of her hips, she caused that cock to slide all the way to the hilt.

A loud groan escaped her lips caused both by some pain but also by intense pleasure. She held her hips up tight to his pelvic bone for as long as she could and then allowed them to settle back slowly to the mattress.

Damion hesitated for just a second and then began to slowly withdraw his cock until it was just at the very edge of Rita's cunt, and then he pushed back in rapidly. He set up a rhythm of slow withdrawals and fast penetration, and within less than a minute, Rita was crying out in passion, begging him to keep fucking her. She had been teased and denied for so long that she had no control over the reaction of her body, and she felt every nerve in her body tense as one and then release. Her cunt began spasming harder than she had ever felt before shaking her entire being. But Damion was far from through, and he kept plowing her faster and faster, and again she began to orgasm. When she was almost so exhausted that she could no longer move her hips to try and match his pace, he finally bottomed out in her cunt and held still. She could feel his cock begin to pulsate, and she knew that he was pumping spurt after spurt and jet after jet of white-hot cum into her deepest recess.

He, too, must have been exhausted at that point because he allowed his entire weight to settle down on her chest. For a little while, that was not too uncomfortable, but soon she began having difficulty breathing, and with what little voice she had left, she begged him to move off of her.

He slowly rolled to one side withdrawing his dripping cock from her snatch. He breathed a small sigh and then climbed up on his knees, bringing his cock to her face. "Open your mouth, slut. You are responsible for this mess now properly clean it off."

Rita was not sure she wanted that nasty thing to pass her lips, but she had no choice. She thought she might be able to resist for a few seconds or even a minute, but he would somehow get her to open her mouth eventually. She was surprised as it slid over her tongue that the taste was not too bad. Her juices had mingled with his, and while his were salty and a little acidic hers were sweet. The combination was almost pleasing to her, and she willingly sucked and lathed his cock with her tongue.

He had been flaccid when he entered her mouth, so there was no problem with him deep-throating her, but the more she ministered to his cock, the harder it became.

"Wow, I didn't think I would be able to get it up again this quick, but you have such a sweet mouth, and you are such a marvelous cock sucker that I think I can go another round. Keep sucking while I fuck your mouth. Try to breathe through your nose as soon you will feel the head of my cock entering your throat, and I do not want you to gag."

He pushed his cock slowly, and soon she did feel her throat begin to expand, and it was all she could do to keep herself from gagging as he had predicted. He held himself completely still for a few seconds to allow her to become accustomed to him, and then he slowly withdrew and slowly came forward. Unlike how he had fucked her cunt, he was very slow and careful as he fucked her mouth, which she was grateful for. It took him a long time, and her jaw was beginning to tire out when she finally felt his cock begin to tense up. She thought that he would cum deep into her throat, but he had other ideas. He pulled almost completely out of her mouth with just the tip of his cock on the end of her tongue when the first eruption came from his balls. A large gob of cum hit her in the middle of the tongue and then another.

"Don't swallow yet he instructed her as he pulled out of her mouth and allowed the last spurt to hit her on her forehead."

As she shook her head to try and keep that nasty stuff from running down into her eyes, he ordered her to swish what was in her mouth around to cover every inch of her mouth and cheeks. Only then did he allow her to swallow.

Rita was exhausted and suddenly depressed as Damion left the room. As she lay there totally and completely humiliated, she heard the door opening, and Loretta stood beside her bed. "I would rather not have to plant a suggestion in your mind to forget what happened here tonight, but I will if I think it is necessary."

"So that is it, right? You hypnotized me and made me want to lick your pussy?"

"Nothing could be further from the truth. I did hypnotize you, but the only suggestion I gave you was that you were tired and wanted to take off your clothes and lie down for a nap. Once you woke up, everything else you did was of your own accord. And I have to say I was indeed grateful for the way you licked my pussy. God, you are one great cunt lapper. I am going to take a chance that I normally would not do. I am going to untie you and allow you to get in the shower and clean up. When you come out, we will talk further."

Rita almost ran for the shower when her bonds were set free. She did not even wait to test the water, and even though it was a little too hot, she allowed it to clean away all the sweat, grime, and cum that was on the outside of her body. There was little she could do to erase what was on the inside, however.

Finally, wearing just a large soft towel wrapped around her middle, she came out of the bathroom. She could smell cigarette smoke in the air, and she was surprised, as she did not realize that either of her sexual partners smoked. Normally she thought that she would have smelt it on them since they had been in such close proximity to her.

Rita had not smoked a cigarette since she had been in college. But after the sexual ordeals, she had been through; the thought struck her that she would indeed like a smoke.

Walking out in the main room, she saw Loretta seated on the big sofa with her legs pulled up under her. She had a small bottle of liquor in one hand and a cigarette in the other. Her face looked peaceful and happy as she took first a sip and then a drag.

"I haven't smoked a cigarette in years, but somehow I have a craving for one," Rita remarked. "Would you allow me to smoke one of yours?"

"No, but I would be glad to share." She then patted the sofa beside her in an invitation for Rita to join her.

Rita had no idea what the woman meant when she said she could not have a cigarette but that she would share. So many strange things had happened to her tonight, and she thought about what could be wrong with one more, so she sat down beside Loretta. She watched as the older woman took a fresh menthol cigarette from her pack and put it between freshly painted lips. For some reason, Rita found that to be erotic and she couldn't wait to find out what would happen next. Loretta took a long drag from the cigarette, sucked the smoke deep into her lungs, and then pulled Rita's lips to hers. Rita opened her mouth and gladly accepted the second-hand smoke as it was expelled from Loretta's lungs and into Rita's mouth.

Rita pulled the small amount of smoke into her lungs, and then the cigarette was passed to her mouth. She now understood the meaning of share, and she took a long pull on the cancer stick and sucked it down. Almost instantly, she felt the nicotine hit her system, and she almost forgot to exhale into the doctor's mouth. They alternated this way until the cigarette had burned nearly to the filter. By that time, Rita was so light-headed she was afraid that she would not be able to stand. That, however, was not an option as Loretta pulled her head firmly against the side of her breast and held her there.

"Will you be okay if I allow you to leave here tonight?" Loretta asked her.

"Yes, of course, but do I have to leave? I was kind of hoping we might snuggle together in that big bed. I would love to spend the rest of the night with you when my hands are not restrained."

Loretta let out a little laugh. "That sounds wonderful to me as long as you understand that I do not eat cunt."

"No problem." Rita also laughed. "I can eat enough for both of us."

Chapter Twenty-One - Ray Wants Out

The sun had risen well past the horizon when Rita finally drove into her driveway. As she opened the front door and entered, she could smell coffee coming from the kitchen, and she was thankful because although she had drunk one cup of the hotel variety, it didn't pack near the punch of the kind they made at home.

She had gotten little sleep the night before, and she was feeling in need of a jolt of caffeine as she walked in and poured herself a cup.

She was just taking her first sip when she heard a noise behind her. Swiveling her head, she saw her husband standing in the doorway, and she could tell by the look on his face and the stance of his body that the man was not too happy.

"Dear God!" He exclaimed. "You look like hell, and you smell like a dirty ashtray. What in hell has happened to the woman that I married?"

Rita did not answer immediately. She wanted to arrange her thoughts in some logical way before committing herself to something that she could not take back. She might have been successful if Ray had shown a little more patience and a lot more restraint. But that was not the case.

"Answer me, goddamn it!" He blurted. "I think I deserve an answer as to where you were and what you were doing out all night?"

"The only thing you deserve is to be on the receiving end of a horsewhip. You gave up any rights to know what I am doing or whom I am doing them with when you decided to stick your cock inside my sister's cunt. And besides, I believe I called you last night and told you what I planned to do. That was more courtesy than you ever gave me before you had a session with Charlene."

"Well, in any case, I have decided that I want out. I want out of this stupid arrangement, I want out of this cock cage, and I want out of our marriage."

"You need to understand that we agreed, and I plan to hold you to it. You have another two weeks left."

"I did not agree to become your cuckold."

"You agreed to do everything I say for 30 days."

"So sue me. Good fucking luck finding a judge that will hold me to a contract that was entered into under the threat of blackmail."

"Speaking of that, do you forget that I still have that video?"

"I am not forgetting anything, and the thought of you sending anyone I know a video of me licking your boots while I jacked off is terrifying, to say the least. But I also know that threat is only good until it is used. After that, you have nothing left to hold over my head. You might want to hold onto it for use at a later time."

Rita was shocked. She could not believe that this was the way it would end. After talking with all the other women, she was sure that Ray would knuckle under just like all the other husbands had. And especially when she had that tape of him licking her boots. But he was right; she couldn't use the tape more than once, so if he was bound and determined that he wanted a divorce, she might just have to let him go.

Ray was studying his wife's face, and what he saw made him just a little sad. She stood before him, and from her demeanor, she was a broken woman.

"I know this isn't fair." He began. "I violated a sacred trust, and you allowed me to set things straight. True, it was a chance to humiliate and demean myself, but it was more of a chance than I am giving you. I am not like you, Rita. You have the capacity to forgive even if perhaps you don't forget. I cannot do that. I will never be able to rid my mind of your voice on the phone last night, telling me that you intended to fuck another man."

"So, where do we go from here?" Rita asked with a note of sorrow in her voice.

"I will be moving out of the house for the present. Once I have retained a lawyer, we can get together to talk about an equitable division of assets. We live in a community property state, and we do not have a prenuptial agreement, so most everything will have to be sold and divided equally. There are always a few things of sentimental value that have to be hassled over, but I am hoping that you will be reasonable."

Chapter Twenty-Two - Living Alone

The first few days were hard on Rita. If it had not been for her work on her book, she probably would have gone stir-crazy. But she still had information to gather even though she was more skeptical than ever about how the hotwife lifestyle worked for the different couples.

She had gone back to talk with Monica again, but most of the talking had been about what went wrong between her and Ray. Monica insisted that Rita not give up, as there was always hope that Ray would spend time thinking and figuring out that he would rather live with a hot wife than a cold one.

And in the meantime, Rita should spend as much time as possible satisfying her urges.

And then, one day, Rita was going through her purse and found the card that Carmen had given her. She remembered that she had been invited to call for a time to interview Carmen's cuckold husband, Harold. So with nothing better to do, she picked up her phone and made the call. She got Carmen's voicemail and left a message saying she would like to set up a time to come by.

A few hours later, her phone rang, and she heard Carmen's voice on the other end. "How about Friday evening at about 7. I have a date that evening, but you are welcome to come by and talk with Harold. I am sure he would be glad to have the company instead of doing one of the lists of chores I normally leave him when I go out. If you get there just a little before 7, I will still be there to introduce you and get you started on the right foot."

Rita readily agreed and made a note on her calendar. That Friday, Rita spent a little extra time preparing herself for an interview with another woman's husband. She carefully chose her clothes so that she would not look sexy in any way, realizing that even if Carmen were going out with another man, she still might be a bit jealous if it appeared that Rita was tempting the one she was leaving at home.

She decided instead of a dress that she would put on a professional pantsuit and low-heeled shoes. She put her hair up in a bun as she knew that when she wore it down, she usually attracted quite a lot of male attention. She applied very little eye makeup and just a touch of light pink lipstick. When she looked in the mirror, she was satisfied that she looked as far from being a hot wife as possible.

She had punched the address into her navigational system and checked how long the drive would take, so she arrived just five minutes before the hour of seven. True to her word, Carmen met her at the door. The woman looked like she had dressed to thrill. Her waist was so small that Rita knew immediately that she was wearing some type of waist cincher under the sheer blouse she had on. She was sure that if the light were just right coming from behind her, she would be able to see the undergarment through that blouse.

Carmen's skirt came just above the knee, but it was so tight that Rita knew that if she sat down or bent over it would ride up, revealing the garters that no doubt held up real nylons. She wore a pair of ankle boots made of black leather and with an exceedingly high heel. This made her black nylon-clad legs look like they had been toned from hours of exercise. Her eyes were accentuated with enough mascara to make them stand out even though they were already extremely beautiful. And her lips were painted the brightest shade of red that Rita could imagine. It was obvious that the woman had applied some gloss as well and those lips looked like they had just been moistened with her tongue.

"Wow, you went all out for this guy. He must be something special." Rita said.

"Truthfully, this was all Harold's work. He is an expert in dressing me for these dates. I hope it was worth his trouble. This is the first time I have ever been with this male. Sometime when we have more time, I will tell you about how I met him and how we hooked up. Right now, come on into the house, and I will introduce you to Harold and let him know that he can tell you anything that you ask about."

Rita had not been expecting to see Carmen so decked out, and she was shocked when she saw her husband. It was not so much that he was wearing a French Maid's uniform, as a lot of the males in this lifestyle were required to dress in feminine attire. Monica had explained to her that males, dressed in female clothing were usually far less aggressive. What did surprise Rita, though, was that Harold was not alone. An older woman sat in a big easy chair while Harold sat on the floor across from her.

"Rita, I want you to meet Harold's mother. She usually comes over and sits with her son when I am going to be out all night. You see, I cannot trust that he won't find a way out of his chastity device and so he has to be tied down to the bed before he goes to sleep. Harriet, this is Rita, and she will be asking some rather explicit questions about how Harold and I live our lives. If you would rather not be in the room while that is going on, Rita can take Harold down to the playroom in the basement."

"Oh, fiddlesticks, girl!" Harriet exclaimed. "You know that I am in complete agreement with how you treat my boy. I was kind of looking forward to watching his weekly discipline session tonight, but I guess that will have to wait until another time."

"Well, I am off to see the wizard, and I hope he is as big in real life as what I think is behind the curtain."

"Have fun, Carmen, but be careful. I worry about you when you are starting with a new male."

"I will, Mom, goodnight all." And she turned to leave.

When she had exited the house, I turned to Harriet. "I have to tell you I am surprised that you approve of the way Carmen treats your boy."

"I have to admit when I first found out I was a little shocked. But, when Carmen explained that Harold had become addicted to masturbating, I understood her need for other men completely. Once a man gets hooked on pulling his wiener, he gets selfish. After just a little while, he becomes almost worthless for a real woman. Premature ejaculation they call it. I call it; they don't give a shit for their partner."

"So how did you find out in the beginning?"

"Well, I came over one Saturday quite by chance to discuss something with Harold. I don't even remember what it was at the time. I rang the doorbell, and when no one came to let me in, I took the key they kept under the matt and opened the door myself. Imagine my surprise when I saw Harold all decked out in his maid's uniform, vacuuming the stairway rug. I gasped and called him a few names that referred to men who like other men, and just then, Carmen came into the room, drying her hair with a big towel. She looked first at her husband and then at me and gave me a big smile. I guess I should explain what she said, and she led me into the kitchen and poured me a cup of coffee while she started to tell me about some changes she had made in her marriage. Harold, of course, was mortified and tried to go up to change back into his male clothing, but Carmen wasn't having any of that. She came dragging him into the kitchen by his ear lobe and forced him to sit down on the floor by her feet while she told me the story.

Well, as soon as I heard that he was addicted to playing with his pecker, I knew that she was doing the right thing. But, you see, she had not gotten him into a chastity tube at that point, and so she had to supervise him almost 24 hours a day. A psychologist suggested that she get the tube. I can't remember her name, but she was a very pretty dark-haired woman."

"Dr. Marks, I presume." Rita filled in for her.

"That would be the one. That woman performs miracles. You know, after just one or two sessions, Harold was a completely different man. He went out and bought that tube himself, although he did get one that was way too easy to get out of. Once Carmen found out that he was secretly unlocking himself and playing with it while she was gone, she got one that he couldn't get off. But she still does not trust him 100%."

Rita looked over at Harold and saw that he was holding his head in his hands in shame. "Look at me, Harold. Is that the way it happened, or do you remember things a little differently?"

"Well, I don't think it is quite as cut and dried as Mom tells it. Sure I masturbated occasionally; every man does. But I will say that I was not as attentive as I should have been. Carmen tried to talk with me about it, telling me that she was not satisfied in bed anymore, but I wouldn't listen. What man likes to hear that he can't get his wife off in bed? Well, one day we had a big argument, and I said the stupidest thing that any man has ever said to his wife. I said if you think you can find someone better in the fucking department, go ahead and try. Sorry for the bad language, Mom. But Carmen told me to tell it as it happened."

Rita couldn't help but chuckle at the obvious lack of comfort Harold was experiencing telling his story in front of his mother. "So, I imagine you were kind of shocked when she came home from her first extramarital affair and told you what had happened."

"Oh, she didn't tell me the first time it happened or the second or the third. She always led me to believe that she was going out with her girlfriends, but it became obvious that something more than that was happening when she would come home smelling tobacco when none of her friends or she smoked. And then there were the birth control suppositories I found in her drawer. I know that I shouldn't have been snooping, but I had to know what was going on. When I found those rolled up in her socks, I thought I would die."

"Why was that so unusual if I may ask?"

"When we were first married, we both decided that we did not want children and so I had a vasectomy. She had no reason to have any method of birth control."

"Wow, so I suppose you confronted her as soon as she came home that time?"

"Actually no, I didn't. I just kept snooping every time she went out of the house. I noticed that the suppositories would almost disappear, and then more would show up the next day. So I started doing the laundry so that I had a reason for checking out her panties, and sure enough, they were always crusted the day after she had gone out with "the girls."

I would never have confronted her at all; I don't think. It was easier thinking about what she was doing than actually knowing what she was doing. But then one night she came home smelling of booze and cigarettes. She was pretty tipsy, and I tried to help her to bed. Well, I guess the alcohol had loosened her inhibitions up a lot, and she pushed my hand away and started to tell me exactly what she had been doing. 'You know what I did tonight, Harold.' She started. 'I got myself royally fucked. Remember when you told me if I could find someone who could satisfy me better than you go for it? Well, I have been going for it, and guess what? I have found ten men that can satisfy me better."

"Oh, my that must have hurt you to the core," Rita stated.

"You are right; it did hurt but not as bad as what she did the following night. She was getting all dolled up again, so I figured that she was going out with another man. I had almost accepted that fact, and I figured that I would just watch a little TV and maybe have a beer or two while she was gone. But then the doorbell rang, and when I went to get it, there was a big muscle-bound guy on the stoop. I asked him what he wanted, and he just shoved me out of the way and walked in. I was pissed, and I told him to get the hell out of my house, or I would call the police. But just then, Carmen walked into the room took this lout into her arms, and started French kissing him. I could hear them sucking on each other tongues, and I wanted to crawl into a corner and die.

Carmen looked at me, and when she saw a tear in my eyes, she started laughing at me, telling me what a poor excuse for a man I was. She then ordered me to get them a couple of drinks and then go up and turn down the bed covers for them, as Michael would be spending the night. I could either sleep in the guest room or on the sofa as long as I kept quiet and didn't disturb them. I can tell you that it was the longest night I had ever spent up until that time."

Rita looked over at Harriet to see her reaction to the story, but she was busy knitting something and didn't seem to be paying either of them any mind. "Don't mind, Mom, none. She heard this all a long time ago. She took it badly at first, thinking that I had married a slut, but when I finally concluded that this was all my fault, she began to understand, and she made up with Carmen. They have been best of friends ever since."

"So tell me. Exactly how was it that you came to understand that it was all your fault?" Rita already thought she had a good idea, but she wanted to hear his take on the matter.

"Well, we were getting along really rocky, and then one day Carmen suggested that we could either get a divorce or we could go to counseling. Well, I still loved her, so I chose the latter. It was the strangest thing that has ever happened to me. As you mentioned earlier, the therapist was Dr. Loretta Marks. When I walked into her office, the first thing she told me to do was to sit on the floor beside my wife's feet. I couldn't believe she said that but for some reason I couldn't argue with that woman. She talked to us about how important good sex was in a marriage and intimated that if the male partner could not satisfy his wife, then she should be free to find someone who could. Well, the first session ended with me still being adamant that if Carmen was going to fuck someone outside of the marriage, then she should at least have the common courtesy to do it away from the house so that I didn't have to meet the other man.

The second session started with Carmen talking at length with the Doctor by herself. When I was finally asked to come in, Carmen left me alone with Dr. Marks. Truthfully I have no idea what we talked about, but by the time I left, I knew beyond a shadow of a doubt that it was my fault that Carmen was having sex with other men. Although I still hated the idea, I gave Carmen my blessing and told her that I would be glad to do anything to make her male companions comfortable when they came to the house. Before you know it, I was helping her get ready for her dates, buying her sexy lingerie, and even giving her manicures and pedicures."

"So when did the chastity device come into play?"

"That happened after another visit to Dr. Mark's office. It seemed that one of Carmen's lovers didn't think it was fair of me to want to have sex with my wife. He suggested that I get a chastity device and wear it to make sure that he was the only lover she had. Well, I balked at that, of course, but then back, we went to the therapist, and on the way home, I stopped at an adult novelty shop and bought my first cage. Of course, you heard that I made sure I could get out of the thing. I was feeling pretty good about being an escape artist. That is until Carmen caught me the first time. Worst beating I ever took. After that, she got a very secure system and forced me to put it on and give her the keys."

"Tell me, do you ever get to masturbate anymore?"

"I used to. Carmen would allow me five minutes to unlock when I took a shower. As long as I could orgasm and get clean in that time, she didn't care. But then I got complacent, and I went over my time limit by a couple of minutes. That was the last time I ever had a real orgasm. She does milk me occasionally just to keep everything working properly. And sometimes she takes a strap on to my ass, which hurts like hell, but it does cause a little seminal fluid to leak out."

"That must be difficult for you?"

"It is especially when I have to help her bathe before a big date. She insists on my washing her hair and her back and even trimming her pussy when it needs it. Once in a while, she even has me shave it for her. That is torture. It is torture because the chastity tube she got for me has sharp tacks in the tip. Of course, there is no way that I can shave her pussy without getting a hard-on."

"So, is everything okay with you two now? Have you gotten completely comfortable with her bringing men home?"

"Yes, although I am going to have a problem shortly."

"Why is that, what more could you have to endure."

"Carmen says she wants me to prove my devotion to her by doing something that I will find extremely hard to do."

Rita looked at his mother and saw that the old woman was now sitting straight up in her chair and listening to every word that was being said. Harold noticed that too and hesitated to continue his story.

"Tell the woman, you damned sissy!" His mother railed.

"She says if I love her I should do the part she doesn't care much for. She never did like sucking cock, but each new man seems to want that as part of the package. So she wants me to do the cock sucking while she does the fucking. And since I will be getting cum direct from the spigot as she calls it, I should be willing to do cleanup duty after they are through. I dread the next time she brings a man home with her."

Chapter Twenty-Three - One More Story

Rita met Milton Townsley through his wife at the Hot Wife Club. She had agreed to be interviewed, but only if her husband was present and could contribute to the story. Rita readily agreed as she found the husband's perspectives to be even more valuable than the wives.

They met at the Townsley's home in one of the suburbs of the city. After seeing so many men serving as their wife's maids, she had almost expected to meet another adorned in a dress and heels. She was quite surprised to see the door opened by a fairly handsome man wearing casual men's clothing. He held out his hand, and she accepted it, receiving a firm but not bone-crushing grip. He introduced himself to her and asked her to follow him into the living room.

His wife Beverly sat on the big sofa that dominated the room, and Milton escorted Rita to one of the equally plush large armchairs that served as an accompaniment. Only when she was seated did Milton go and sit next to his wife. He immediately put his arm around her, and it reminded Rita of how she and Ray had sat together early on in their marriage.

They carried on some small talk for a little while with Rita telling Beverly how much she liked her home and the arrangement of the furniture and art that hung on the wall. They even talked a little about the weather and how unseasonably warm it seemed. But as with all the other interviews, eventually, the conversation had to evolve into the Hot Wife lifestyle. And Rita was happy that Milton was the one to bring it up.

"I know that you didn't come here this evening to talk about the weather, although that is by far the easier conversation to have. Beverly tells me that you are writing a book about women who cuckold their husbands, and since I guess I fit into that category, you would like to ask me a few questions. Is that about right?"

"Yes, and I am even more curious now that I have had the opportunity to see the two of you interact with one another. You seem so comfortable with one another and frankly not at all what I expected."

Beverly smiled at Rita and cocked one eyebrow a little to show her curiosity. But then her husband broke in before she could voice the question that her face plainly showed she wanted to ask.

"I think I know what you mean. I have spent quite a lot of time perusing websites that deal with cuckolds and their dominant wives. In most of them, the husband is either dressed as a French Maid or as a little girl in sissy clothing and is groveling at his wife's feet. Was that kind of what you expected when you came here tonight?"

"Well, I have to admit that I have seen quite a lot of that since I started this book. But in every house, there is always something a little different. However, in almost all of them, the wife is the dominant member of the duo. You two seem like you are more on an equal footing."

" I am the submissive," Beverly stated. "I only do what Milton tells me. If anyone sits at the other's feet, it is I., But most of the time, we spend our time together like this. I am most happy when it is just the two of us together, sitting quietly with his arm around me, letting me know that he loves me beyond anything else."

"So, where does the Hot Wife angle come into play?"

"I like to watch." Milton simply said.

"I am not sure I understand. You like to watch what?"

"I like to watch Beverly having sex with other people. I knew that she was submissive when I first met her. That was the reason that I started dating her. I wanted someone who would allow me to dominate and humiliate them. I know that sounds incredibly cruel, but I want to be completely honest with you from the beginning so you can understand how we got to our present point."

Rita turned to Beverly and asked. "Do you have to get your husband's permission to speak?"

" I usually refer to him as my Master, but he has already permitted me to answer any questions that you might have for me. If he thinks it will embarrass me, he would enjoy it even more."

"Okay, then did you know from the very beginning that he was only dating you to have someone to abuse?"

"I don't know if I knew that from the very beginning, but it didn't take me long to catch on. I think on the second date when he began to unbutton my blouse while we sat in a booth at a busy bar, I had a good idea that he wanted to embarrass me. Of course, I objected and tried to remove his hands from my buttons, but when he told me if I did not obey him, he would pull me over his lap and spank me right there I allowed him what he wanted. But of course, if we had been somewhere in private, I would have provoked him to spank me. God, I love it when he uses those big hands of his to warm my bottom. Anyway, he did not just stop with the buttons on my blouse. He opened four of them and then reached inside and pulled my breasts out of the bra cups. For a brief instant, anyone in that bar that was looking our way and a great many of them were, could see my nipples before he allowed the blouse to close back up. But even then, the only part of my breasts that was covered at all was those now rock-hard nipples.

We sat there for the rest of the night like that drinking and talking as if nothing had happened. And then a strange man came over to the booth and spoke directly to Milton, ignoring the fact that I was even there. He asked Milton if it would be all right if he danced with me, and Milton readily agreed. He turned to me and said, 'Show the man a good time.' So I started to button my blouse, not wanting my bare breasts on view for everyone in the bar, but Milton told me no. He did not threaten or raise his voice. He just said no, and I knew what he was referring to. So I got up moving as carefully as I could, hoping that my blouse would not fall open, and walked with a man I had never met to the dance floor.

It was a slow song, and he immediately pulled me tight against him. He didn't even begin with his hand on my back but immediately moved it down to the swell of my ass cheeks. He openly massaged them through my skirt as he dry-humped me on the dance floor for everyone to see. About halfway through that dance, he pushed me back a little bit and, with his other hand, pulled my blouse fully open, allowing my tits to come completely out in the open before pulling me back against his chest. Now the only thing between my nipples and his chest was his shirt. I was mortified. I wanted to crawl under the table and hide, but that wasn't going to happen anytime soon. Between dances, he would not let me return to the table. He kept one hand on my elbow while his other hand began unbuttoning his shirt. When the music started to play again, he pulled me back against what I now knew to be a very hairy chest so that my bare breasts and nipples were pressed against all that hair. And you know what the strangest thing was? Not a soul complained about the half-naked man and woman swaying to the music.

So finally, he took my hand and led me back to Milton. He watched me as I slid into the booth, his eyes devouring my legs as my skirt slid up them. Finally, in a voice loud enough to be heard at the next table, he said. 'That is one hot slut you have with you. I would like to fuck her sometime if you don't mind. I expected Milton to get angry and punch his lights out, but that didn't happen. Instead, he handed the guy his phone and told him to program his number, and Milton would give him a call and set it up.

I was dumbfounded. When the guy went back to the bar, I turned to Milton and demanded an explanation. For Christ's sake, he hadn't even fucked me yet, and he was offering to allow some other guy to do the job. 'You don't expect me to fuck some stranger, do you?' I demanded. All he said was, 'I expect you to do everything I tell you and without argument.'"

"Wow," Rita said. "I can't believe that you just didn't get up and walk out on him. And you, Milton, weren't you surprised that Beverly didn't put a stop to your antics at that point?"

"No, I knew that she wanted the humiliation as much as I wanted her to have it. What she didn't tell you is that after I opened her blouse, I also reached beneath the table and pushed one of my fingers inside her vagina. She was gushing wet, so I knew she was as excited as I was."

"So go on, tell me what happened next."

When the bar finally closed and I had been forced to dance with a dozen other men, Milton led me out to his car. I thought for sure that he would allow me to button my blouse now, but again he said no. He then told me to pull up my skirt take off my panties and give them to him. I was now bare-chested and bare-bottomed, but at least I still had my skirt to cover my pubic area with or so I thought. Before he would allow me to buckle my seat belt, he made me pull the bottom of my skirt up and tuck it into the waistband. I figured that would not be too bad since it was pitch dark outside with no moon to light the night. But before we started to pull out of the parking lot, he turned on the dome light so that not only could people in high-profile vehicles see my cunt, but they would be attracted to look our way because of the light. At the first red light, we came to he rolled down my window so that anyone pulling along my side of the car could yell obscenities my way. Halfway home, I started to cry. I could not believe that any man could treat any woman that badly on a second date.

Milton turned his head and looked at me when he heard me sobbing. 'That is good. Let it out. I love to see a woman with tears streaming down her face. Well, I made up my mind right there that this would be the last date I would ever go on with Milton Townsley."

"But it is obvious that it wasn't or you wouldn't be here. So why did you go for a third date?"

"Well, he dropped me off at the curb in front of my apartment. He didn't even bother to walk me to my door. But he did command that I not adjust my clothing until I got completely inside. I was still only halfway to the building when he drove away."

"And at that point, you were still determined not to ever see him again?"

"Yes, but there was a slight problem with that. Once I got inside, I ran to get my vibrator out of my vanity drawer. I was so damned hot and wet that I had barely turned it on when I began the most violent orgasm I had ever experienced. It seemed to go on and on forever little tiny aftershocks following the main volcanic eruption. Unless you have experienced something like that, you cannot understand how addicting it can become.

Well, I managed for a couple of days before I realized that I wasn't ever going to be happy without Milton in my life. So I finally got up the nerve to call him and ask him if I could see him again. He was quiet on the other end of the phone for a while, and I figured he was thinking of some excuse for not seeing me again. But then he spoke to me. 'I have a poker game on Friday night with some of my friends. We need someone to serve drinks and keep the snack bowls filled. Be here at eight sharp, and you are not allowed to wear a bra or panties. I prefer my sluts to wear garters and real stockings and make sure that your blouse is see-through and that your skirt is short enough to show the ends of your garters.

I started to object, but he quickly told me that if I said even one more word, then I could just stay home and not bother to show up at all.

When Friday came, I looked through all my clothes to see what I might have to wear, and I discovered that I didn't own anything that would be revealing enough for what he had described. So off shopping, I went spending money that I needed for other things, on clothes that I figured I might never wear again. I finally ended up going to one of the stores that specialized in slutty clothing and got a blouse so sheer that you might as well not even have one on and a skirt so short that if you bent over in it, your entire pussy would be visible. To top it off, I found a red pair of heels with a six-inch heel.

I knocked on his door five minutes before 8. A man I hadn't met opened it. He took a long time looking me over before inviting me in. I could feel his eyes boring into my ass as I passed him. Milton barely looked up before pointing towards the kitchen. 'Everything is in there to make the drinks and bring in a couple of bowls of pretzels and popcorn for the guys. Get a pad and take their drink orders. If there is anything too exotic for you, there is a laptop computer on the counter so you can look up the directions.'

I found a pad went back into the living room and asked the guys what they wanted to drink. Thankfully no one seemed to want to test me out, so their' orders were easy to fill. I made sure to get extra tall glasses so that I wouldn't have to run back and forth all night. They, too, seemed to appreciate that as it gave them more time to gawk at my assets. But then finally one of them complained that I was standing too close to them and that I might be getting a look at their cards. So Milton told me to go over to the padded bench at the very side of the room. It was sitting with the long way pointing back at the card table. When I got to it, he told me to bend over and lay down on the bench from my waist up. I was now facing away from everyone in the room, and of course, my cunt was on display for everyone to see. I heard several comments about how good my pussy looked, and then I heard Milton say, 'Well if you like it that much, sit out a hand and go fuck her.'

I was dripping wet, and I am sure they could smell my sex even though I was several feet away from them, so when the guy walked up behind me, he didn't even feel to see if I was ready. He just plunged his cock to my Dr. Marks introduced herself and then got straight to the point. "Your wife has told me about a special need she has, and she tells me that you are unwilling to help her with it. Is that true?"

"If you mean has she told me that she needs to be beaten when we make love, I find that to be beyond anything that a normal person would be able to help her with."

"Then she has no other alternative but to go out and find someone else who will satisfy that need. Are you okay with that?"

"No, of course, I am not okay with that. We are married, and she took a vow to keep herself only unto me until death do us part. I forgave her the indiscretion she committed with her brother-in-law, but I am not going to condone her finding another man to have a kinky affair with."

"Then I will recommend that she retain a good divorce attorney and kick your ass to the curb. You cannot have it both ways. You are going to share in her pain and pleasure, or you are going to be looking for another wife. Perhaps you can find one that fits your normal expectations. So is that what you want? Because if it is, I will make a phone call right now so she can file the proper forms."

"What in the hell kind of a therapist, are you?" Jason railed.

"The kind that does not believe in putting up with male bullshit. None of this is your wife's fault. Every ounce of the blame rests firmly on your shoulders."

"I don't understand what it is that you want me to do?"

"I don't give a damn what you do. It is your wife that needs your compassion. I have already told her that I think she should be looking for someone who loves her enough to help her with this need. You notice that I do not call it a problem because it is not. I can give her the names of a dozen sadists that would be glad to use their whips on her back while they stuff her cunt with a cock that I am sure is much bigger than yours. Of course, the other option would be for you to stop at an adult novelty shop and pick up a good flogger to use yourself."

"I wouldn't know where to begin, even if I did decide that was an option."

"Well, why didn't you say so if that is all you need is a little instruction? I am an expert. How about it Charlene, are you up for a little show and tell?"

"What do you have in mind, Doctor?"

"First, tell Jason what it is that you want from him. And tell him in such a way that he will understand."

Charlene turned to her husband, and in the firmest voice, she could muster announced. "Jason, I want you to whip me while we are making love."

"Charlene, is that really what you meant to say? Did you want to use the words making love?"

"No."

"Then what word did you want to say?"

"Fucking," Charlene said in a soft voice.

"Speak up, slut. I don't think Jason heard you."

"I want you to whip me while we are fucking. Jason, did you hear me that time?"

"So, Jason, now you know what your wife wants. Are you willing to give it to her if I show you how?"

"I will try."

"Good, Charlene, take your clothes off and go bend over that padded bench. I know you would probably prefer something less comfortable, but I guarantee you that you will be in a great deal of pain soon. I am going to hurt you. I am going to hurt you very badly. Is that what you want?"

"Yes."

"When you address me, you will call me Mistress. Do you understand slut?"

Charlene was surprised that she did not take offense when the Doctor used such a derogatory word to address her. She felt her pussy beginning to respond, and she relished hearing even more such words.

"Yes, Mistress, and thank you, Mistress, for recognizing that I am indeed a slut."

Charlene was completely naked and bent over the padded bench, and Jason just stood there fully clothed. "Well, aren't you going to take off your clothes as well, Jason? You can't very well fuck your slut wife if your cock is still covered by cloth."

"Why do you keep referring to Charlene with such ugly names? She is not a slut, and I don't think you are helping her by taking away what little self-respect she has left."

"Charlene knows that she is a slut, and she craves being called a slut. Give her a dollar before you fuck her, and then we can call her a whore. Now get your clothes off, or should I get my strapon?"

Reluctantly Jason began unbuttoning his shirt. Next, he undid the button on his trousers and pulled the zipper down. Finally, he stepped out of his shoes so that he could get his pants off his legs.

"The undershorts as well." The Doctor instructed.

Carrying a heavy flogger, she directed Jason to stand right behind his wife. "Guide the tip of your cock into her cunt and then thrust forward with everything you've got."

Tired of arguing, Jason followed instructions. He didn't even check to see if Charlene was wet. He just drove straight to the hilt. As his hips hit her ass cheeks, Dr. Marks swung the flogger as hard as she could against Charlene's shoulders. The woman let out a scream causing Jason to pull out and step back.

"Get that cock back inside her. She didn't tell you to stop."

"But you hurt her. She can't possibly want anymore."

"Tell him, bitch. Tell him what you want."

"Oh, God, please hurt me. That was so wonderful. Jason, please fuck me while my Mistress whips me."

"You will be the one who decides when the whipping stops Jason." Dr. Marks told him. "When I see cum running down her legs, then I will stop whipping her."

And again and again, the whip rose and fell. Charlene did not scream after the second stroke, and by the tenth, she was moaning but in obvious pleasure. And Jason had got himself into the mood as well. He couldn't believe how good it felt fucking a helpless woman while she was being severely whipped. When he had finally expelled the last drop of cum from his balls, he stepped back just enough so that his spunk could run out of his wife's body. Only then did the whip stop rising and falling. His wife's back was crisscrossed with vicious red welts.

Jason started to turn away but then decided perhaps he was still due something for his aggravation. He grabbed his wife by the hair and pulled her to her feet. When she was standing, he forcefully turned her until she was facing him. Putting one hand on each of her shoulders, he forced her to her knees. "Suck my cock, cunt. And make sure that you swallow every drop of my seed that I ejaculate into your mouth."

Charlene was the most willing cocksucker that Dr. Marks had ever witnessed.

"I think you two are going to be all right. Just make sure you stop and buy that whip on the way home. And while you are in there, get a few pairs of alligator grip nipple clamps. Take Charlene in with you, and I bet she will see a few other toys to take home as well."

Jason turned to Dr. Marks. "Thank you so much for this gift you have given us."

"Oh, it wasn't a gift. Wait till you see my bill. You will be the one in pain then."

She showed Jason out of her office, but she held her hand up in a stop sign position to let Charlene know that she wanted to talk with her in private. When the door had closed behind Charlene's husband, Dr. Marks turned to Charlene.

pubic hair and began rapidly sawing in and out of my tunnel. I did not expect him to shoot his load that fast, but I had barely begun to feel the tingles of my first orgasm building when he shot a huge load of spunk deep inside me. He didn't say a word to me as he pulled out and then wiped his wet sticky cock on the side of my skirt.

I started to stand to leave the room to clean up, but again Milton just said one word, 'no.' So all I could do was continue to lay on that bench with cum running down my legs. It wasn't long before someone else positioned himself behind me and pushed his cock inside me. Again no attempt was made to make sure I was satisfied as again within a minute he too exploded inside me.

The guys enjoyed me so much that they even got their drinks and snacks to keep me in that position. Of course, after a little while, my legs began to cramp, and I started moaning. Only then did Milton himself come to me, and that was just to tie me in that position so that I could not get up until he freed me. That he did not do until every one of his friends had fucked me several times, and my legs were so knotted that when he finally released me, all I could do was drop to the floor.

He gave me a drink of soda, and although I wanted some strong liquor, he wouldn't allow it. He told me that since I had to drive home soon, he did not want to be responsible for my driving drunk. As soon as I was able to walk on my own, he pointed to the door and told me to leave. I was devastated. I could not understand why I would have gone through all of that and then just be summarily dismissed. I was again crying as I reached the door.

As I was opening the door, he finally spoke to me. 'I won't be seeing you again for a while. In the meantime, you are no longer allowed to wear panties except for when you are having your period. And you are never allowed to wear a bra.'

And I did not hear from him again, but I did hear from every one of the men that had fucked me at his house that night. Each one wanted a return session with me, and I refused them all. There was now only one cock that I lusted after, and that was the one I still had not experienced, Milton's."

Rita now addressed Milton. "This has to be the most bizarre story I have ever heard. I guess I can almost understand why Beverly did it. She was addicted to being controlled. But what did you get out of it unless you were masturbating while your friends fucked your date?"

"What I found exciting was the fact that she would obey me without so much as a murmured complaint. And I specifically told the guys that when they fucked her that they were to use her, not pleasure her. I wanted to see how much she would allow to happen.

And then I told them to give her a call and ask if they could have another go at her. I was very pleased when she turned every one of them down.

I was now satisfied that she would do almost anything that I told her. There was only one other test that I wanted to put her through. I had become good friends with a very cruel woman I had met at one of the clubs. I asked Beverly about how she felt about having sex with another woman, and she told me that it was not something she had ever done, nor did she want to ever do it. So, of course, the next time I invited her over, Charlotte was already there waiting. She was sitting in one of the chairs in the living room with her legs spread and no panties on. Other than that, she was completely dressed. I did not even introduce Beverly to her; I just told Beverly to get on her knees and begin licking Charlotte's cunt."

"I think I would like to hear this account from Beverly if you don't mind."

Milton did not reply; he simply nodded in the affirmative to his wife.

"Hell, I was scared to death. I had never been with a woman, and I didn't even know what I was supposed to do. Oh sure, he had told me to lick her slit, but how that was supposed to go, I didn't know. But with my face bright red with embarrassment and my gut clenching, I got to my knees and crawled to the woman. I tentatively took a sniff to see what I would be tasting, and Charlotte started laughing at me. It is kind of ripe, isn't it? I have been saving it for you since Milton told me he wanted you to learn to lick cunt. After all, what fun would there be in that, if it smelled all rosy and sweet? Insert your nose between the folds and get it coated with all that slime. And then get to licking. Start at the very bottom and run your tongue up to my clit. Push your tongue as deeply as you can into the bottom and then repeat the process.

My stomach started to roll after just the first swipe and how I kept it from spewing I have no idea. It must have taken that woman a good hour before she finally gave way to her orgasm. By that time, my tongue felt like all the cords had been stretched to their limits. My face was completely coated with pussy juice, and I was not allowed to wash it off before I was sent home.

That was the most horrible thing that had ever happened up until that time. Of course, I have had any number of lesbian encounters since, and I have learned to thoroughly enjoy the taste of a good clean pussy."

"After that, I knew that Beverly was the woman I wanted to spend my life with. If she could not complain about what I had her do with Charlotte, I figured she would do anything I asked of her. So the next day I called her and asked her to marry me."

"And you still had not had sex with her?" Rita asked.

"I have never had sex with her. You see, I am unable to attain an erection or to ejaculate. On our wedding night, I sat in the corner while my brother consummated our marriage with Beverly. She and he have become quite close over the years, and at least once a month, I have him come over and spend an entire night with her. I spend that night in the guest room, and it gives me great pleasure to hear her screams of pleasure as the bed bounces against the wall. We are even thinking about having a baby with my brother as the father. I am a little reluctant to allow that to happen because once we bring a baby into our home, it will dampen some of the kinky things I can make her do.

But I know she would be a great mother. And that is one decision that I am going to allow her to make all on her own. If she wants a child, all she has to do is stop taking her birth control pills and have Russell move in until she knows she is pregnant.

There you have it, what else would you like to know?"

Rita looked at the woman in the room. "You mentioned that you would have loved for Milton to spank you early on in your relationship. Does he do that often?"

"Spanking no, whipping yes. And even that he leaves it up to someone else, his sister quite specifically. She is as cruel as he is kinky, and she loves to work my back over with a riding crop. And she knows that I get sexually excited from being whipped on my buttocks, so she never strikes me there. But she sure knows how to light up the backs of my legs and my shoulders. And of course, she then gets excited at what she is doing, and she insists that I use my tongue to bring her off. And usually, before she leaves, she tells me to kiss her boots. Once, she even made me lick them clean. Although the leather didn't taste bad, the rubber soles were disgusting. I am glad that she doesn't get off on me doing that for her."

"Yes, sweetness, but now that I know you do not enjoy it, I may put the word in her ear. You may be licking a lot of rubber soles soon. You would like that, wouldn't you?"

"I would like anything that gives you pleasure, Master."

Epilogue

At the conclusion of that interview, Rita had all the information she needed to write her book. It still took her quite a while to put everything together in a useful form. Even when she was finished, she did not send it to her publisher, as she was not sure what Ray was planning if he filed for divorce.

And then, one day, she received notice by certified mail that Ray had indeed filed for divorce. She found out a little later that he had tried to file on the grounds of adultery, but in the state, they lived in the only real grounds for divorce were irreconcilable differences.

A date was set for a hearing before a judge. Her attorney informed her that normally that was just a formality. In 99% of the cases, the judge would just ask both parties if they believed the marriage was irrevocably broken and then grant the divorce.

But for every rule, there is an exception. As Rita walked into the courtroom with her attorney, she was not completely sure what to expect. Within a few moments of her sitting down, the court was called to order, and a very distinguished older man in a black robe took his seat behind the bench. The case was called, and then the judge got right to the point.

"Mr. Talmadge, you have filed for divorce from your wife of a little over five years. Is that correct?"

"Yes, your honor, I have."

"And do you believe that this marriage is irrevocably broken, Mr. Talmadge?"

"I do your honor."

The judge held up his hand in a stop sign motion. "I do not want to rehash what you believe did or did not happen to get to this point. Mrs. Talmadge, do you believe that your marriage is irrevocably broken?"

"I do not, your honor!" Rita said emphatically.

"Since there is a disagreement between the parties as to the state of the marriage, I am not going to rule on this petition today. Instead, I am ordering the two of you to get marriage counseling. Until the therapist gives this court a formal recommendation, this divorce proceeding is on hold. Mrs. Talmadge, since you are the one who still holds out hope for this marriage, the bailiff will give you the name and number of a counselor who has proven to be very successful in resolving these types of issues. The court is dismissed."

It took two months for the first session to be scheduled. Rita arrived right on time and was pleased to see that Ray was already there and waiting for her. She went to the receptionist signed some forms and produced her ID to be copied and kept on file. She then went over and sat close but not next to her husband.

"I still believe that we can work this out between us, Ray." She said.

"And I am firmly committed to living the rest of my life without you in it. So let's get this charade over with."

It was a few minutes later when they were called into the inner office. A tall-distinguished dark-haired woman met them just inside the door. She held out her hand first to Rita. "You must be Rita. I am so happy to meet you." Then she turned to Raymond. "And I presume you are Raymond. My name is Dr. Loretta Marks. I will be trying to help the two of you work through some problems that I understand you have. Ray was heading for his seat, so he did not see the doctor give Rita a little wink of the eye."

Then Ray turned back to her. "Your name is Marks?" He asked. Loretta simply nodded at him, and he continued. "Haven't I heard something about a Dr. Marks? Why do I know the name?"

"I suppose it is possible that you might have heard of me. It is, however, highly unlikely that you would know me personally. Most of the males that come into my office don't even remember they have been here once they leave."

She then sat down directly across from them and crossed her legs. As one booted foot began to swing seductively, Ray could not take his eyes off of it. Within just a few seconds, he was mesmerized, and his eyes became heavy.

The end.

I want to thank you for reading this story. I hope you enjoyed it as much as I did writing it. If you have comments that you would like to make, please feel free to email me at wandapeters1@yahoo.com

I have other books that you might like. Below you will find a list:

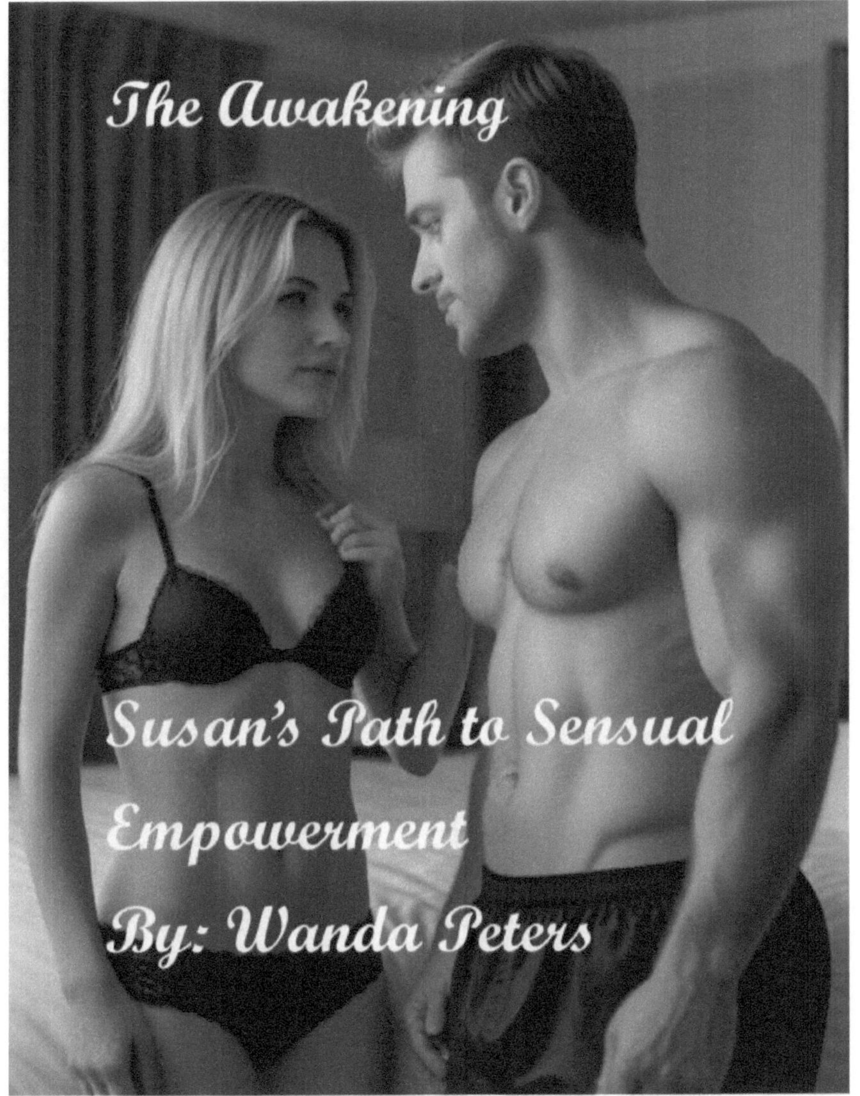
The Awakening
Susan's Path to Sensual Empowerment
By: Wanda Peters

My
Evil
Step
Sister Returns
Illustrated
By: Wanda Peters

Embracing
My
Inner
Bitch
By: Wanda Peters

Bound
For
Desire
By
Wanda
Peters

An Interview With
An Erotic
Writer
By: Wanda Peters

An Old
Flame For
Ava
By:
Wanda Peters

Don't miss out!

Visit the website below and you can sign up to receive emails whenever Wanda Peters publishes a new book. There's no charge and no obligation.

https://books2read.com/r/B-A-COFL-KFTGB

Also by Wanda Peters

10 Reasons You Should Cuckold Your Husband
Cruel Wife, Slave Husband
Embracing My Inner Bitch
Erotic Short Stories of Dominance and Submission
My Evil Step-Sister Returns Illustrated
Cuckolded By A Stranger, An Erotic Novel
Cuckolded By His Boss
The Hot Wife Club
Cuckolded and Bound for Punishment
Cuckolded By My Best Friend
Cuckold's Anonymous
An Anniversary To Remember
My Wife's Surprise
Terrified of Bondage A Wife in Peril
Training Her Cuckold Husband
A Little Devil in Georgia
His Mother's Advice
Addicted To High Heels or A Slave To My Wife's Boots
The Huntress
A Wedding to Remember
Evil Under a Western Sky
The Number Four Reason You Should Cuckold Your Husband
Cuckolding The Bootlicker
Bondage and Discipline 101
Tales of Love Romance and Marriage

Tales of Love, Romance and Marriage
The Evil Therapist Returns
Cracks in the Vow Six Stories of Love's Demise
Two Books Of Domination And Legal Thrillers
An Old Flame For Ava
An Interview With An Erotic Writer
Bound For Desire
The Awakening- Susan's Path to Sensual Empowerment

About the Author

I have been writing erotica for the past 15 years. Most of what I write is about dominant wives and submissive husbands. Occasionally I will write a book about a submissive woman because that seems to be what some readers want.